ARE YOU AS SENSUALLY AWARE AS YOU SHOULD BE?

Every male has the ability to enjoy a rich, satisfying sensual life. But a lot of men are shortchanging themselves when it comes to tapping their sensual potential.

THE SENSUAL MALE is a guide to increasing sensual awareness. Dr. Lichter, a well-known practicing psychologist, has written down in clear, everyday language how you can add unsuspected new depths to your sensual experience.

MAN

THE SENSUAL MALE

by Dr. Sigmund Lichter

AN ORIGINAL HOLLOWAY HOUSE EDITION
HOLLOWAY HOUSE PUBLISHING CO.
LOS ANGELES, CALIFORNIA

PUBLISHED BY
Holloway House Publishing Company
8060 Melrose Avenue
Los Angeles, California 90046

First Printing 1970

Printed in the United States of America

About the Author:

Dr. Sigmund Lichter has many years of experience as a psychologist in private practice in New York City, and he has also found time to serve as a consultant to several school districts, to teach at the college level, to assist at mental health clinics, and to join the staffs of a number of hospitals across the United States.

He received his B.A. degree from Brooklyn College in 1952 and his Master of Arts from New York University in New York City in 1953. He obtained his Doctorate in Psychology from the University of New Mexico in Albuquerque, New Mexico, in 1964. Among the many licenses, certificates and credentials presented to him are Private Practice Psychologist License, School Psychologist License, Marriage, Family and Child Counselor License, and Teaching Certificates empowering him to teach at any level through Graduate School.

Dr. Lichter has written many articles and psychological studies for professional journals in the fields of psychology and other social sciences. This is his first book written for the general public.

CONTENTS

INTRODUCTION

by Dr. Sigmund Lichter

The luckiest man in the world today can be you, just to be alive in this new age of sexual freedom, and that applies whether you are sixteen years old and have stolen this book from your father, or if your hair is gray and you still yearn to fulfill young sexual fantasies.

No other facet of human life, including space travel, has experienced such explosive advancement as the expansion of male and female sensuality in the last decade. To reach the moon, when it has been a goal for centuries, is a relatively easy thing. To reach the heart of man and break through to his innermost desires, when they have been denied, blockaded and condemned for centuries, is a major accomplishment.

For most of the life of most people, we are locked within ourselves, and it is only in love and the expressing of it that we are able to reach out and touch another human being and then withdraw again. What could ever be more important? Is it more pleasurable to you to watch a ship travel to Mars and back, or to try to establish contact with life on earth? Which sounds like more fun?

Each man possesses a different degree of sensuality, which is not the same as saying some guys are hornier than others. Your sensuality reflects your outlook on life and your over-all personality. There is no innate sensuality drive. Males have sensual equipment. To choose not to use the equipment is a choice each man has to make, because sensuality is learned, not instinctive. To cultivate it the only required skill that you must possess is the ability to change.

For the past half century, discussion of sensuality, its causes, and development, have been dominated by what has been termed the "puritanical" approach. Within the past decade a new approach has been emerging, and finally we can present in a book the rather novel concept that sex is fun, which is something that everybody who ever tried it has known all along.

The new trend, moving away from repression of sensuality and toward more explicit expression of it, is an honest one, based on human feeling. Those who deal in human behavior are beginning to recognize that the ultimate goal of each individual is a high degree of sensual competence. Since we all seek to make our lives as pleasurable as possible, it is natural that the sensual route be taken. It is equally natural that sensuality should be developed to utilize the male's freedom, uniqueness and potential.

In selecting the area of male sensuality for this book, I had two reasons. First, while it would be naive to assume that all behavior can be described satisfactorily in terms of male sensuality, it is equally naive to assume that sensuality is something to be carried out exclusively within the confines of a bedroom. Second, in spite of the surge of emphasis on practical methods of developing sensuality, the direct techniques of achieving sensuality are in danger of being overlooked.

So, what we have here is intended to serve as a guide or manual for males on how to increase their sensuality within a short span of time – as short a span as it takes to read this book, in fact. Also, the fairly sensual female may find the book usable for aiding her in improving her relationships with males. Primarily, the text is designed to "stretch" the sensuality of males and give them a deeper understanding of the personality dynamics of their fellow human beings, male and female.

The suggestions and techniques presented in this book grew out of the author's belief that we no longer need hypocrisy in our feelings and ideas about sensuality, thus many people will find the material "daring" and, perhaps, "shocking." Many excellent works exist in this field, but they are primarily concerned with the general area of sexuality or sensuality for the female. Others are too highly technical and some are written only for their erotic value.

Some words and graphic descriptions used in this book may be considered by a few people to be vulgar or obscene. They are not used for eroticism or shock value, but because they convey most explicitly the intended meaning. I believe that the freedom to use words that are emotionally explosive should be exercised when emotionality is required.

Sensuality is nothing to be ashamed of, and it is not "dirty." At its best, it can be the highest achievement of the human being, and it is the most human thing that most people experience in their entire lives. Still, there seems to be some conspiracy to keep people from fully developing and exploring their sensuality, to the extent that most people have one vocabulary for their private lives and thoughts and another one for public use. You can find out everything you want to know about the inside of your car, but when you try to find the most vital information about your body and the expression of desire, you are considered somewhat obscene for even being interested.

But if we are to fulfill our desires, we must look for the facts. It's a matter of emotional and sexual success that is at stake. I do not mean sex in the narrow sense of taking a penis and inserting it in a vagina but in the much broader aspect of sensuality. There's no physical or mechanical way to sexual happiness that does not bring the mind into action as well. Sensuality is deeply rooted in the emotions, love in particular. The best and most infallible aphrodisiac is love.

The sensual male is in love with all females. What kind of man is the sensual man? Is it a matter of physique or stamina? Can intelligence help in sensuality? Can sensuality be utilized in strange as well as in familiar surrounding? Can we find a way to use our sensuality without fear? Do males differ from females in sensuality?The answers to these questions, and many more, are all contained within.

If you believe as I do that sex is fun, then this book also will be an entertaining experience.

CHAPTER I

IS YOUR SEX LIFE NORMAL?

It is a constant surprise to find out the many ways by which people adapt their sexual needs to their life situations and the stresses and problems they encounter in living. One person who considers himself "average" enjoys sex once a month, while another person who may live in the same neighborhood and move in the same circle of friends considers himself sexually deprived because he only goes to bed with a woman twice a week; he, too, calls himself average, and indeed who is to say what is average? But if our sexual practices vary from one man to the next, the mental adaptation to the need for sexual release takes even stranger forms.

There is a woman who comes to me for therapy who spent the first six sessions outlining to me the wide-open, come-one-come-all sex life she led. She would pick up men and have intercourse with them, alternating with oral sex, on and on until her energy alone endeared her to them so much they wanted to keep her. At that point she would go out and make the rounds with someone else. Then she would bring the two men together and take them both on, either in a sandwich—one man behind her penetrating her anally while the other faces her and inserts himself in her vagina—or by bringing one to orgasm orally and having vaginal intercourse with the other.

The capriciousness and wantonness of her love-making, and her memory of every detail, was astounding, and ostensibly she was talking about different men each week when we met. It seemed to me that she was, either by dint of an over-active imagination or through the accomplishment of a deliberately flagrant sex life, trying to shock me. She was an attractive woman who would have no trouble finding willing partners for her activity, and she was not a shy person, pulling her chair right up to my desk and looking into my eyes as she related her "shocking" sexual exploits to me. Nothing she had to say did particularly shock me, of course, but I encouraged her to talk, impatiently wondering how long she would delay bringing up her problem, which manifested itself in fits of depression due to sexual conflicts inside herself, I was to discover later.

Finally, one week, instead of sitting down right in front of me and resuming her verbal salvo of sexual experience, she sat on the far corner of a couch in the most distant part of the room, hanging her head and stammering out only a few words, speaking so low that I could hardly hear her. My impression was that she had finally done something which was truly shocking, but after all that she had described, I racked my brain wondering just what it could be. She started off, after considerable struggle, saying, "I didn't want to tell you this—" What, what shuddering thing could she have done that was so terrible that someone as bold as she should sit there, practically hiding? Finally, she got it out, declaring as though she expected the ceiling to fall in. "I masturbate."

Believing this to be the prelude, by way of clearing her throat to start another one of her stories, I waited for her to continue. But no, that was *it.* She had laid half of the population of the state, but to her, the idea of masturbating was something so terrible she could hardly talk about it. Somewhere in her formative years she had "learned," or convinced her own mind, that sexual promiscuity was all right, perhaps even healthy, but the girl who masturbates is some sort of pervert skidding to hell on wheels.

Sexual problems are a major source of disorders in almost every field of medicine and social behavior. Despite the changing nature of law and custom, and the more open attitude about discussing sex, there are as many taboos, confusions and uncertainties as ever. Because of some quirk in their sexual "learning" process, or due to some great trauma or fears, people are forced into strange attitudes toward various facets of sex, and therefore also into strange methods of finding sexual release.

Most of us have heard about little old men sitting in their automobiles on the street, looking for girls with big breasts—breasts that resemble their mother's—and masturbating there daringly, almost in public. But the same men would flee in terror if a real flesh and blood woman came over and offered to perform precisely what their fantasies dictated.

Some men need to "rape" women in order to successfully achieve erection and release. In happier arrangements of this enactment, the men actually find girls who will accommodate them by acting as though they are resisting, struggling in pain until the man by sheer force of masculine strength overpowers them, plunges his organ into them and stabs and stabs away unto release. The men who do this actually are so unsure of their male sexuality that it will only work for them like this, when they come on like Hell's

Angels, terrifying their helpless sex partner by their sheer brute manhood. They love to tie up girls, too. Still, it can be an adjustment to a deep-rooted problem that otherwise could become criminal if enacted without the permission of the rapee.

There are men who whip women, drawing blood across their bare backs with stinging lashes of cord or rawhide, or even, sometimes, with special velvet whips. Women willingly submit to this, too, and vice versa, apparently according to some law of love that declares that for every sadist there's a masochist, and within every masochist there is a sadist. In extreme forms of this, painful mutilation, burning, slashing and even death occur by overstepping the limits of pain or violence, and again we have a criminal situation. Men seeking their mothers mate with big fat women who have huge breasts and an authoritarian, disproving manner, who take the complete initiative in the sexual experience. Or having a very harsh father, they dress up or have their partner dress in rough masculine materials and accessories, the belts and whips and leather symbols, and enact a scene of sexual discipline in which one partner must under threat of bodily punishment perform whatever demeaning sexual task the other commands.

Man is a socially created animal and society is doing a poor job of creating a proper psychological climate for man's sexuality. For every so-called "weirdo," environment is the greatest molding force, causing the stresses to which the persons react. Man can change, and man does change as he grows to and through maturity. But man lives in what amounts to a tension system like a bridge slung on cables so that its own weight helps keep it up. Everybody lives with a state of tension within himself and further tension exists in his relationships to all other individuals. Life itself is a tension system, and the interplay between these tensions and the individual self makes a man what he is and what he does. Nobody exists as a single person, although many try, only to beat their heads and their lives to a pulp against the brick wall of frustration. The single, individual personality only exists in relation to others.

One man who came to me for therapy had what we might consider a way-out, perverted manner of sexual expression. First of all his sex life was most difficult because just about the only place he could carry out sex on his terms was in the shower. Surprisingly, although we should learn never to be surprised at anything in humanity, he did find women to participate. Naked, the two of them would get into the shower. He would lie on the floor and she would urinate all over him. *Then* he could get an erection and reach orgasm. That was the only way. What the little charade was saying to his unconscious mind was, "I know I am worthless, so worthless as a person that the basest of human functions should be performed on me," and some men require further demonstration, requiring someone to defecate on them before they can perform, a perversion called scatophilia. The idea of the thing is that by urinating or defecating on him, you were agreeing with him, admitting he was worthless, but still accepting him. If this could be, then he could perform sexually.

Of prime importance to sexuality and the way it manifests itself is the way in which the human being develops in his early infancy, childhood, and adolescence. From the moment of birth man is in contact with other personalities. Somebody slaps him on the ass to get him breathing, others stay around and keep him alive by sticking things into his mouth. There is always, all through life, some interpersonal relationship being carried out by all persons, and these interpersonal relationships are the basis for sensuality. The interaction even can be between fictional or fantasy creatures or things, but they are there; for example, the solitary man who masturbates while dreaming that some sexy movie star is manipulating or otherwise exciting his penis.

Every man, as he grows and learns, develops his own system of tension within himself to regulate what is harmful and keep it out. If he sees too much harm, too much threat, the tension becomes too great and he withdraws into a shell of security; sometimes the tension is so great and he hides so successfully that he is actually removed from himself. People say "He's out of his head," and it's so. The self-system, which has the serviceable aim of reducing tension and anxiety to make life more pleasant, can be employed to too great an extent or encounter too great a tension, causing an emotional "coup" or abdication, eventually taking over the personality or actually becoming the personality. This self-system, having no insight or self-corrective powers of its own, concerns itself only with preservation of itself and effectively eliminates the man who devised it. The result is a split personality.

In the same way that there are endless gradations of sexuality, there arc also endless adjustments made by people attempting to live without being hurt. Not all men can be unafraid.

Earlier it was mentioned that there are cases where men whip women or degrade them by dominating them and abusing them and when we hear of such cases we may either experience a vicarious thrill or sneer at these "monsters," or just shake our heads at how sad it is to see such "weirdo" practices arise. On the other hand, to a lesser degree, most of us have experienced some occasion in our passage through life when encountering the warm, naked female form, we either are unable to attain erection, or we attain it and ejaculate prematurely, both of which often are the hidden mind's way of avenging anger at the female.

Most of the so-called perversions are present in varying degrees of compulsion. There are exhibitionists who expose their genitals in the streets, and there are more adaptable ones who become topless, bottomless go-go-dancers, sex film performers or just nudists. And there are probably just as many voyeurs as exhibitionists, most of them paying admission to live sex shows or films, or daring to watch exhibitionistic women undressing without pulling down their shades. There are narcissists who love only themselves but find ways to display themselves proudly and women to bow and adore them without requiring mutual affection. There are perverts who pursue coprophilia, love of dirt, perhaps licking dirty toes and osmolagnianists who are aroused by the odors alone, but who has not been stirred to some degree by a perfume or aroma of sex itself? Homosexuals and lesbians abound, and pederasts, but then there are many "normal" men and women who have tasted vaginas or penises or anally injected their wives.

There is bestiality, intercourse with animals (of all horrors!), and there are shy, lonely old widowers who live on farms and have sexual arisings. Fetishists have sexual intercourse with shoes or lacey panties or hosiery, but some women of the sexual living dead rival these inanimate objects as inactive participants. There are nymphs and satyrs and may they find each other. And there are sad cases of unnecessary chastity and platonic love. The weirdos are not so weird. They are all humans trying to reconcile fear and desire. What's so odd about that? Especially when so many "normal" people let their sensuality die by default, or never try to fulfill its potential?

There is an expression, from an old Latin motto, "Nothing human is foreign to me," and a more popular one, "There but for you go I." So, much of our sensuality and its manifestations depend on our adjustment to the pressures of life. If the distance between the daily functioning of the male and his inner feelings continues to widen, then a schizoid condition develops. Those who are able to attain real sensuality are those whose inner feelings and outer activities are in tune. Since so much pressure, repression and positive horror surrounds the development of sexuality, it is no wonder that we have so many kinks in the expression of sex.

One of my patients described a girl who was unfortunately frigid but had made a remarkable adjustment to her condition. Her condition, actually an inability to perform freely in bed, enjoying herself and giving joy, was obviously due to having her tender sensibilities of awakening womanhood crammed with the horrors of hell. Inside her mind she was living with the "knowledge" that sex is filthy, animal behavior which marks any girl among the damned, and yet she had these feelings which came from her body which seemed very good and cried for exploitation. Her solution to the conflict can be described briefly. She let him strip her in her apartment and lay out full length on her bed, but she was as rigid and unyielding as stone, the muscles of her face and her groin contorted into full tension. She recoiled from every caress. He found it impossible to force his penis into her and she wouldn't even unlock her legs to the prying of his tongue.

Recognizing the conflict, and spotting an obvious velvet drapery tie, handily slung over the headboard of the bed, he took it and wrapped it around her wrists securely, tying them behind her back. Immediately she began thrashing with her whole body, almost apoplectically. Her flesh was transformed before his eyes from cold marble into vibrant warmth. Kneeling at her head he thrust his penis at her lips and she shook her head violently, resisting, but before he could move away, she opened her lips to it, parted her teeth and dived on it like a cobra. He fondled each breast and the nipples stood up rigid as though on command. Stroking her crotch made her hips swing like a piston at his hand. There was no caress that didn't arouse her now. There was nothing he couldn't do to her, and she was already coming from the frenzy of her own wild movements at the instant he put himself into her, and she kept coming until he did, one of his rare experiences in mating with a perpetual orgasm.

It was so satisfying a completion for him that he just lay there for a long while, softening, reluctant to withdraw while she snuggled close and subsided like a red coal burning out. In the quiet acceptance of one another that usually follows such activities, she confided to him that unless she had had a lot to drink, that was the only way she could really enjoy sex, tied up. However—again demonstrating the amazing ability of the mind to adapt—she usually carried in her purse, in case of emergency, a pair of handcuffs!

This kind of restraint is one manner of coming to terms with one's unconscious, which prohibits sex. After all, if somebody ties her up, she can't help it, can she? As long as she was able to make that concession to her unconscious, she was able to run wild with emotion.

Restraints and bondage can be subject to a complex variety of interpretations, depending on the people who use them. Often a girl is placed completely in chains, spread-eagled on the bed so that she really is powerless to move yet wide open physically. Or her hands are tied over her head with soft rope, or handcuffed there, while her legs are spread apart by being tied to opposite ends of a broomstick at the ankles, exposing her crotch. In some cases, the idea of restraints like these is for the male to practically torture the girl with stimulation. He teases her clitoris, fondles her, brings her to orgasm again and again, driving her to new heights of sexuality until she is pleading, begging and crying for him to please put it in, please. When he does enter her, the female's magnified arousal makes all the more man of him, which is the aim of this little body game—a way of reassuring his secret doubts about his erection, his thermometer of manhood.

In summary we might ask, what is normal sexual expression?

In the name of sexual adventure, almost anything which is not painful could be tried by willing partners, and in fact might be recommended, for the one basic law of sensuality is that the more a person practices sex, the more it is heightened. It is not something to save up for a sexy day. Like good deeds, the more you do the better it is for you, and the more it makes you want to do. Only when some isolated variation of the male-female sexual possibilities becomes an almost exclusive substitute for the intimacy of sexual communication might one be in trouble; then the person should perhaps pursue a frank analysis of his behavior before going over the deep end. But if your sex life pursues a goal of sexual communication, rather than avoiding it, you are headed in the right direction.

CHAPTER II

TEST YOUR OWN SENSUALITY

Are you sexy? How sexy? How do your sexual feelings, and the expression of them in action, compare with those of other males? Your sensuality is a natural talent. Do you ever wonder how effectively you are using it? Even though you may have made an introspective study of yourself, your personality and attitudes, and probably have taken an IQ test and possibly even had your horoscope charted, there remains one essential facet of your existence which, like most people, has been neglected. Your unique sensual vitality, your sexual potential, can be measured.

The sexual quotient scale, familiarly called S.Q.S., is a test for revealing some of the dominant sensuality, techniques, emotions and complexes in your sexuality. Special value resides in its power to be useful for all males between the ages of 18 to 65. It is relatively short, easy to score, and capable of assessing various aspects of sensuality so that change can be quickly detected. It should be kept in mind that the climate of public opinion in this country is such that testing sexual ability is not generally regarded as an area for psychological diagnosis. The state of our present ability to diagnose sexual prowess is so shoddy, in fact, that no possible avenues should remain unexplored merely because of theoretical bias. Each new technique deserves to be evaluated in its own right, rather than rejected untried. The purpose of this sensuality scale is just to begin, to help you begin to look at your sexuality more objectively.

The scale is divided into three sections: Sensuality, Technique and Emotionality.
Note that the statements all refer to yourself in terms of what you are doing now, the way you behave and feel today, not what you *can* perform. For each item circle the one of the four answers that is closest to how you are actually functioning at this time, even though the replies are not exact in each case.

Do not answer with what you think would be the approved attitude of society or anybody else, but search your own mind and memory for your personal response. There are no "right" or "wrong" answers; your sensual profile should provide clues for you concerning the possibilities that lie ahead. Consider each answer as a measurement of the degree of your reaction, responding to the extremes of left or right when you are very decisive about what you do or do not do.

Proceed without fear. There are questions to which only a very limited number of people will reply "always," but the test aims to examine the whole extent of the human sexual experience.

SEXUAL QUOTIENT SCALE

Think about each question and choose the one of the four answers that is closest to how you feel at this stage of your life. Please place a check mark next to the word that comes closest to how you do things at present, although it may not fit your distinct preference.

1 - I take female friends to "adult" movies with me.
Always___ Often___ Sometimes___ Never___

2 - I use aftershave lotions and body lotions.
Always___ Often___ Sometimes___ Never___

3 - I can tell the difference between songs such as ballads, rock and roll, country and western.
Always___ Often___ Sometimes___ Never___

4 - I use coarse language such as the words "fuck, tits, balls, cunt, ass" during sexual activities.
Always___ Often___ Sometimes___ Never___

5 - I like to eat raw clams, whipped cream and/or barbequed foods. (Two out of three qualifies.)

Always___ Often___ Sometimes___ Never___

6 - I can distinguish the odors of different perfumes that women wear.

Always___ Often___ Sometimes___ Never___

7 - I like to use my tongue in kissing.

Always___ Often___ Sometimes___ Never___

8 - I can feel the difference between velvet and silk cloth with my eyes closed. (If in doubt, test yourself on this one.)

Always___ Often___ Sometimes___ Never___

9 - I enjoy teasing a girl's nipple orally while having intercourse.

Always___ Often___ Sometimes___ Never___

10 - I like to view the body of my sex partner.

Always___ Often___ Sometimes___ Never___

11 - Outside noises distract me if I am making love.

Always___ Often___ Sometimes___ Never___

12 - I enjoy giving and receiving oral sex.

Always___ Often___ Sometimes___ Never___

13 - I feel that sex should be limited to the bedroom.

Always___ Often___ Sometimes___ Never___

14 - My idea of a good party is one at which I get something going with an interesting girl.

Always___ Often___ Sometimes___ Never___

15 - I enjoy the idea of going around nude in the privacy of my house.

Always___ Often___ Sometimes___ Never___

16 - I have a greater sex drive than the average male.

Always___ Often___ Sometimes___ Never___

17 - I would prefer being good in bed to being the most successful person in my field.
Always___ Often___ Sometimes___ Never___
18 - Sex novels turn me on.
Always___ Often___ Sometimes___ Never___
19 - I like to vary sexual positions.
Always___ Often___ Sometimes___ Never___
20 - I like to experience sex with a group of females, in reality and/or fantasy.
Always___ Often___ Sometimes___ Never___
21 - I am aggressive when making love.
Always___ Often___ Sometimes___ Never___
22 - I prefer to initiate sex action with a girl.
Always___ Often___ Sometimes___ Never___
23 - When I choose my clothes, sex appeal is the prime consideration.
Always___ Often___ Sometimes___ Never___
24 - I need sexual preliminaries to get me in the mood for sex.
Always___ Often___ Sometimes___ Never___
25 - I don't feel nervous and shy around women.
Always___ Often___ Sometimes___ Never___

To show you the meaning of your answers, the test has been broken down into three sections which we translate into Body Awareness, Sex Activity, and Feeling. On the proper lines below, put your score for each question, then add up each column separately. In scoring, each of the twenty-five questions should be counted as follows:
Always_1_ Often_4_ Sometimes_3_ Never_1_

	BODY AWARENESS	SEX ACTIVITY	FEELING
Question:	2____	1____	3____
	5____	4____	8____
	6____	7____	13____
	10____	9____	14____
	15____	11____	18____
	16____	12____	22____
	17____	19____	23____
		20____	25____
		21____	
		24____	
	Total____	Total____	Total____

Looking at your total in the first section, on body awareness, if you scored between 17 and 32, this is an indication that you have an excellent grasp of your sexual identity as a male and are at ease with your body. You prefer to use your sexual capacity and meet challenges. Women do not find you physically boring. If your total is between 9 and 16, it means that you have a fairly good grasp of your sexual identity and are able to display your body with little or no embarrassment. A score of 8 or less, however, shows that you have some difficulty thinking of your body positively and do not use your body sensually enough.

The second section of the test, dealing with sexual activity itself, is helpful in illuminating some areas of sexuality that create difficulties. A person who is shy and who thinks swearing is vulgar may nevertheless be quite enthusiastic once he goes to bed with a girl. The reverse may also be true, in that the male who is willing to display his sensuality may reveal a wide variety of hangups when it comes to actual lovemaking. A score of 24 to 36 in the second section indicates that you utilize many sexual methods and enjoy the sex act itself. You are open, understanding and sexually knowledgeable. A score from 10 to 23 would tend to indicate that your techniques are rather conventional but adequate. If your score is 9 or less, it would seem that you do not concern yourself sufficiently to increase your passion in sex. Your sexual actions are conservative and inhibited.

The third and final section of the test is to help you take a closer look at who you are and what you like, to discover what you really want, and what you enjoy emotionally. A score of 19 to 32 means that your emotions are utilized well in your sensuality. The score places you in the upper range of emotionality. If you scored from 9 to 18 it suggests that you are about average in your understanding of your sensuality and are open to ideas. A score of 8 or less, however, indicates that you may be a little too uptight about exhibiting your feelings and could use some loosening up.

Now, to examine the totals on the entire

test, the figures you scored must be changed slightly to balance out the importance of one section over another, a system which psychologists call weighting. To obtain your "weighted" score in the first two sections of the test, circle the number in the column at the left which includes your score, and then go across and mark the number in the same line to the right. For example, if your original, raw score in section one is 12, then your "weighted" or interpretive score will be 15.

Body Awareness Raw Score	Weighted or Interpretive Score
25 – 32	25
17 – 24	20
9 – 16	15
1 – 8	10
Sex Activity Raw Score	
28 – 36	50
19 – 27	40
10 – 18	30
1 – 9	20
Feelings Raw Score	
25 – 32	25
17 – 24	20
9 – 16	15
1 – 8	10

You should now have circled three numbers in the right hand column, one for each section of the test. Add the three numbers from the right hand column to arrive at your interpretive score for evaluation of the test results as a whole.

The superior category is a score of between 85 and 100, which indicates an open acceptance of sex and sensuality. You are a connoisseur of sensuality and are a sexually free person. You are friendly, open, understanding and sexually responsive. You are free in your mental attitudes and women find you open and receptive. You have made a major effort to delve into sensuality and have a degree of sensual knowledge few men in our culture possess.

A score of 69 to 84 is in the high average bracket, indicating that you have a liberal approach to sexuality and are not uptight about displaying sensuality. You have confidence in your potential as a male and are at ease with your body. You are very probably a self-starter who is unafraid of life. You are receptive and crave female companionship.

Total scores falling between 44 and 68 still present a picture of a male who is not afraid of his sensuality, but plays the game of sex with a good deal of caution. You are tolerant of your own failings as you are of the failings of others. However, you are somewhat sexually inhibited and tend to use friendship as a shield against erotic involvement.

A definite sensual deficiency is indicated by a score of 43 or less on the interpretive scale. If you fall in this category your attitude typifies pessimism, submissiveness, and a tendency to withdraw from life, or to block yourself from reaching sexual situations where you fear overstepping your emotions or adequacy. Your outgoing impulses and desires are often thwarted by timidity, which makes you prone to involvement in poor sexual relationships.

If you scored poorly on the test, do not mourn too badly, for the majority of males in America are in your category or below. But sensuality is improvable. It can be developed by practice, exercise and learning. Those who have it know that it is a life-enriching quality well worth having. It is not a matter like being born blind or rich or inheriting money, and it is not guaranteed to you like freedom, although the truly sensual man is the only one who is really free.

CHAPTER III

HOW TO BE SEXY

Some men look at themselves in the mirror and decide that their physical self is not on a par with Richard Burton, Robert Redford or similar two dimensional idols and that, in effect, they do not deserve to be laid. This is of course nonsense. It's a sort of cop-out, a reason for not playing. The game is sex and you can be fat and bald and have a face like a bulldog and still be a great lover. It's what happens between the sheets that counts, but since making the most of your appearance can help you get there, the matter of personal appearance is worthy of brief discussion.

The average man looks around the world today and he sees males of that phenomenon called hippies. They violate every precept of masculine attraction, seemingly. They wear long hair that falls in unkempt strands. They dress in what appears to be rags, and you can't tell what they look like because their faces are covered with hair, too. And they have a reputation for bathlessness. Yet, almost invariably, it seems, you will find a stunning young blonde, her long hair falling straight down her back and her face fresh with wonder, hanging on to the hippie's arm. The average guy thinks to himself, I may not be perfect, but I sure look better than that, so how come he's got the girl? Well, as for the disheveled hippies, you will have to forgive them, because they don't know any better: they *think* they are good-looking, and that is the secret.

If you learn to accept yourself as you are, and come to believe that you are truly handsome, then no matter what you look like, you will begin to behave like a handsome person. There are no absolute standards for male beauty, so why should some arbitrary configuration—whether taken from male fashion ads or cinema images—be imposed on you? Especially if it will cause hundreds of women to live their lives without experiencing you?

Actually, by Hollywood standards, it could be said that I myself am not the perfect presentation of human masculinity. I offer the possibility merely for the purposes of conjecture and would not for a minute admit it, of course, without hedging. It certainly is a miracle what a set of whiskers can do.

So take a good look at yourself, not only your face and your physical shape, but the way you carry yourself, the way you walk, the way you comb your hair, the clothes you wear, the expression on your face. Nothing has to be perfect about you, of course, but the principal is this: If you are going to put yourself to bed with a beautiful woman, it is better to be as good looking as possible. After all, you want to go to bed with as fine a specimen of female as possible, so the reaction works both ways.

When you inventory your assets, you must realize that only the most rare of problems in appearance cannot be remedied. It is not our intention in this book to solve each and every problem that might afflict you, but only to make you aware that there is hardly a thing you might not like which could not be changed into a physical asset.

Starting at the top of your head, even if you have the total handicap in that area of being bald, there are several recourses available. First off, why not just shine it? Don't ever forget what Yul Brynner did for the bald men of America. He and many other men without a single hair on their heads have led very interesting sex lives. There are fashion designers, doctors, scientists, cartoonists and even filmmakers who suggest that the man of the future will not let his skull be cluttered with a lot of fuzz, and the barest of domes will be the most popular. This isn't a suggestion to shear off whatever hair you have at this instant, since hair does play a part in sex attraction in the current world.

If your problem—if you consider it a problem it may be a problem—is a lack of hair, there are several ways to farm a new crop. The most obvious of these is to procure a wig. Depending on how much money you can raise, the hair-piece makers of America can put you into a head of hair maybe better than your own—some are even swim proof. It would amaze the average person to discover how many famous leading men of Hollywood, with offscreen reputations as great lovers, owned their own hair only by virtue of purchase. It would be simple to mention names, but not so simple to argue with their image-conscious lawyers. You can get full heads of hair, partial hair pieces, patches, and even false sideburns—matching of course—and you can wear them all the time or any part of the time, even to bed with the girls running their fingers through your glorious mop. And if they ask, Is that your own? you can reply, Damn right. You paid for it, didn't you? There are processes such as hair reweaving and transplants which can be investigated, and all such procedures have their merits and drawbacks. Check out any such operation before trying it; ask your doctor; ask people who tried it. If someone offers to regrow your own hair ask him if he also knows how to regrow teeth, especially if the person happens to be bald himself—or wears a wig.

Those who have no worry about the abundance of hair have the options of changing the style and the color to best suit their facial characteristics. Here again is a field for the experts. Invest ten bucks in a hair styling, just to see if you'd like a new look, if something can be done to better become you. If not, you can always comb it back the other way.

If you have a normal set of the rest of your features, you will find directly under your forehead, centered, one nose. There will be cheeks, two eyes, lines of hair above them, lips and mouth, chin, ears. If everything counts out right, you're in pretty good shape. There is no particular deformity of face that some woman will not find cute.

One young man, who had no problem in attracting girls, was disturbed by the fact that his nose looked like he had personally lost every prize-fight in the heavyweight record book. It was broken in a half dozen places and flattened out in a zigzag across both cheeks. The guy got the nose fixed up through very expensive plastic surgery which made him look like anybody else, and for a while he was proud of his new looks. But it seemed after the initial newness wore off that he had lost something. The girls were no longer very much interested. What had been an appealing face, with a lot of "character," had been reduced to something just average, something not very special. Girls had always found his smashed face rather cute. They liked it that way.

Once there was a man with such a prominent nose that it interfered with his occupation. He held up banks for a living and his nose was of such singular proportions that he was almost readily identifiable. He solved the problem by wearing to work one large bandage across one cheek or the other. Despite the protruding, obvious nose, all that anyone seemed to notice was the bandage.

This clever ruse may be of limited application, because sooner or later you're going to run out of excuses for wearing bandages. But how about a full moustache instead? Or a goatee—which is also excellent for a receding chin problem, by the way. On the other hand, if thy nose really offends thee, pluck it off, as the bard said. The plastic surgeon will probably say, "That'll cost you a grand." Maybe only half that, and maybe he'll finance it. Or start your own "lay-away" plan—that's what it's all about.

The plastic surgeons, who by the way now call themselves cosmetic surgeons and other more dignified appellations in keeping with their burgeoning business and subsequent wealth, can do things with needles that lift faces, eliminate sags anywhere, puff up cheeks, unbag eyes, improve complexions, remove birthmarks, make scars disappear, all with little more bother and time than going to the barber. Their prices are higher. But don't be afraid to talk to one about some problem that bothers you—a surgeon, though, not a barber.

Are your ears too big? So were Clark Gable's. High cheek bones? How about Jack Palance? No individual feature is objectional of itself, so long as it doesn't bother you. The *feeling* of being handsome or presentable is what is most important here. If you look it all over from chin to the top and have to concede that you're just plain ugly, and you can't take a certain pride in that, then hide. A beard may be the dressing for you. If you grow a beard full enough, all the girl will ever see will be your eyes, and presumably your soul will eke out of these and win her.

For those who do interpret their faces as lacking in the ideal characteristics for the attraction of the female, a beard or moustache might be just the right touch to bring out all the hairy masculinity within. Before acting on this, approach the task with clear-headedness. After all, you've got a set of disorganized whiskers on your crotch, and that's not doing you any good. A pattern is called for, a different one for each man.

While letting your beard grow, observe other men with beards. Clip pictures of men with beards. Think about beards. What would you be most comfortable with? Choose a pattern you think you'd like and sketch it in ink over your photograph. You may spoil a lot of old photographs before you get it right, but the old photos won't be any good anyway after the beard is added. Who'd recognize you? Choose your adornment and trim away.

One little matter before proceeding to the physique. Complexion is important. A good, clear complexion exudes good health and creates a favorable impression. Unless there is some complication which is in the province of a doctor, then diet is the key to a good complexion. Knocking off junk foods, the high-sugar snacks, candy and soda pop often is enough to clear up a blemished skin, but if there is some acid imbalance beyond this minor restraint, see a skin specialist and ask for a diet of proper foods. Stick to it and there'll be changes. Or, of course, in addition to the hundreds of creams and other medications, you can resort to a tan. No sun? How about sunlamps? Put one in your bathroom and you'll get a good facial tan in just the time it takes to shave.

Now comes the physique. If you dare, and you must sooner or later, take your clothes off and look it over critically. After all, this is the body you will have to ask if some lovely girl would like to have lying on top of her. Overweight is often a bugaboo. You don't have to be a shining, oiled, rippling paragon of muscles but rings of flab and/or protruding fat should be eliminated. There is a diet for every man to achieve his proper weight, and there are special exercises for every spot on the body that may be out of trim. Get a book or join a gym or join an exercise club and work out regularly. Such a program is desirable not only from the standpoint of personal appearance but also from the point of view of stamina. If you are eating poorly and not getting proper exercise, which are usually the conditions which bring about overweight and the paunchy waist, you're not going to be in shape for all the sex demands that your imagination will be calling for. Keeping the body in good condition will not only help you get into the proper bed, but it will keep you there longer. She won't let you go away.

Now, so far as physical appearance is concerned, we have covered the body from one end to the other and it must be conceded that there is no facet of the human organism that cannot be accepted or changed to achieve the best possible outward look. General good health is the spark required behind it all, and this, barring disease or disability which are unsurmountable, is available to the vast majority of men of all ages. Scientists today are realizing that men of seventy or seventy-five should really be counted as middle aged, because they are actually at just about half of what should be their lifespan. When man stops abusing his body with ill care and eliminates the majority of infectious diseases, the life span will reach one hundred and fifty years, the experts declare. The sensuous male will recognize that by keeping in top shape all the way along, he will be able to double and triple the span of his active sex life. Now that's what I call living.

Whoever it was that said "Clothes make the man" was obviously shilling for a haberdashery, but certainly, since custom has decreed that we do not go forth into society preceded by our most prominent organ in the naked state, clothing and various ornaments do play a vital tribal role. The king is always the most lavishly dressed, with gold crown, cape of fine furs, a throne of velvet and a scepter of gold, but the sex king doesn't have to go to all that expense.

A little good taste will go a long way in the matter. One doesn't dress like a hippie when going to a formal dinner party, nor vice versa, unless the idea is to shock rather than attract and make oneself acceptable. If one dresses like a dirty cowboy, one may find that he only appeals to dirty cowgirls; which is not to be knocked until one has tried it, but affords little variety in life.

They say that when it comes to good taste, one either has it or one doesn't, and to a certain extent this is true. If you don't have it, find somebody who does. If you happen to think that a red tie, a yellow shirt, blue slacks and a blue jacket are sharp when worn together, you may be in need of a friend. On the other hand, in today's loosely dictated styles, you may be a trend-setter. When in doubt, copy or steal dress ideas, not necessarily from your friends, but from people who you know are making out on a level that you'd like to make out on. When it comes to dress it's hard to make any flat statement, even in such limited terms as never wear brown shoes with blue slacks: there may be a whole untapped field of girls who make the same mistake in color clashes, all eminently layable, and liable to be well disposed toward men whose choice of clothes reinforces their own selection. Do try to wear sexy underwear, whatever, and it need not match anything.

Well, you may fix up this body into good shape, clothe it pleasantly or even attractively, and put hair on top, and still you're inactive. Somebody would come along and put a tag on your toe, you're dead. Your appearance includes much more; in fact the expression on your face, the look in your eyes, and the posture you maintain, your way of walking, of carrying yourself, may have more to do with good looks than all the finely chiselled features in a store window dummy.

You don't have to smile all the time, and as a matter of fact I'd frown on that, but if you've got good teeth—and that's between you and your dentist—it won't hurt to smile with regularity enough to display your dental integrity. When a girl sees a man smiling, she thinks he's enjoying himself, and that's what she wants, to enjoy herself, so she wants to be where it's at. It is never necessary to go around grinning all the time, and you may get into trouble if you do, but your expression, even if it takes practice, shouldn't be malevolent or repelling. Even if you've led a rough life and have downturned lines creased all over your face, it doesn't take too much mirror practice to work a firm look of neutrality and noncommittalness which may intrigue some females. They'll wonder if you're stupid, intelligent, angry or philosophical, and if you play your cards right, you'll have their panties down before they find out.

Posture is an important part of a man's projection of his masculinity, but here again there are no hard and fast rules, other than that an obvious erection in a business suit usually turns girls off–*usually.* One need not walk as rigidly as though just graduating from West Point, and if one stands ramrod straight around a party one may find himself being mistaken for a waiter. What seems to be the guideline in posture is that the person's bearing denotes a certain pride in the organism. Even a slouch can be graceful and not unappealing if the position does not display a disregard for the value of the physical being that is there disported.

In other words, if you have a healthy attitude toward your own value as a human being, if you carry your physical self as one would treat a thing of some value, then it will show. You can walk with a casual confidence that is almost the direct opposite of an aggressive stride and thereby exhibit a stronger, more attractive appearance than that stride. It all hinges on how comfortable you are with yourself.

Nothing here is a suggestion that play-acting, adopting this or that manner will be the best for you. All that can be declared for sure is that knowing yourself and your feelings will permit you to carry yourself with respect and command respect for what you are, a human being, a male. Shoulders back, stomach in, one-two-three march—forget it, that's not the way; it's a good way, but it must come easily. The way you move your body, or don't move it, even the way you sit, the things you do with your hands, tell things about you to others; they may not even know exactly what, but they will sense the things that your body is saying.

Nothing has been said up to this point about cleanliness, and it should go without saying that in Western civilization the majority is for it. I'm not in favor of overbathing—running for the shower or a spray can the minute a bead of sweat appears. But on the other hand, how is that cute little girl you have your eye on going to feel when she spots a ring of dirt around your neck or fingernails? Chances are she won't feel inclined to go down on you without further inspection.

But before you dash to the bathroom and douse your cheeks, armpits and toes with the latest concoctions designed to give the impression you work in a florist shop, consider this: While we appreciate pleasant aromas, perfumes and colognes, there are many interesting odors that are indigenous to humans alone. Madison Avenue has completely inundated our culture with the supposed requirement for squeaky clean hair, breath, armpits and even genitalia, the latest scent being one specially made for female crotches.

Which brings up the interesting question, What has been done up to now about pubic odor? Will historians write, "Female pubic odor prevailed over all of America until the last third of the Twentieth Century?" Or will saner nostrils prevail? Of course now they have come up with a male version, but such a whiff seems destined for failure unless the advertising geniuses devise some "gimmick" such as producing an aerosal can that can do double duty as a dildo; then the women will buy it for their men.

It's easy to ridicule such an approach to human cleanliness. In fact, perfume has its origins in the need to cover up malodorous men who bathed so infrequently that a dab of some exotic fragrance was a public service. Going bathless will not improve your sex appeal, but it must be stressed that we should not eliminate from humans all that is human. Some secretions and aromas that are exuded from humans while making love or working up to it can be very exciting.

Which brings to mind a friend who had a very intriguing practice playing upon the sense of scent. He would run a clean handkerchief around his naked crotch at the height of its erogenous state, capturing the odor of maleness at its source, and he would fold that handerchief into a pocket. At the proper moment in an evening, either running his hand through the cloth or the cloth to his cheek, or hand to cloth to hair, he would bring this very personal odor into play, while dancing or conversing with a girl he intended to bed. Now, he never really had to bring up the subject of sex; it was all there, in the air, literally.

After a rousing lovemaking session the abdomens and chests of the participants are likely to be covered with a fine, glistening sweat, and it is probably high on the list of sexual delights to bury your nose and run your tongue over the naval and breasts of your partner. The odor and taste of human love are imbedded in the memory of anyone who has ever experienced it, and evoking that memory can play a significant part in conjuring up the image again and bringing lovemaking to mind—without a word, without a wink, love is in the air.

All of these things the sensual man has,

his face, his physique, his bearing, and even his distinct male odor, which is not to be obliterated by drugstores. There is nothing there which has to be given him, nothing which requires reaching beyond his own self to procure, only requiring the best care and presentation he can provide.

Mention of the tongue brings up another vital male possession, the voice, which is the bridge to extending one's personality and intelligence to another. The voice itself, its tone and inflections rather than the words conveyed, is important in and of itself. Get to know your voice. Learn how to use it. Tape record your voice, saying things you'd like to say, and play it back; listen to what you sound like, because that's what your partners will be hearing. Learn to do things with your voice, with your words. Learn to like your voice, because somebody else will have to like it.

When it comes to personality and intelligence, you don't have to become a conversational master, full of glib, sophisticated comments on every topic that might arise in social circles today, because sex itself is a basic communication—and it can be done in exclamations, grunts and sighs which require no super mentality.

I remember watching a couple at a party one night. The man had walked over to the girl and struck up a conversation which she readily acquiesced in, and he, sensing acceptance, talked on. I couldn't hear what he was saying but the young man had a reputation for being an excellent raconteur. The man talked and the girl listened. However, at a certain point, the girl just excused herself and walked away. Later I talked to her briefly and mentioned seeing her reject my friend earlier. She said, "He's very nice, but I felt like saying, I don't want to talk, I want to make love!"

And most people do. However, that example is an extreme one, as rare as that particular girl. One cannot just walk up and say, "Hello, I'm John," zip, "and this is my penis," even though such directness might be the ultimate honesty. Because let's face it, it will add immeasurably to your own pleasure and successful conquest once you can learn to reach out to your partner, to care what goes on in her mind and body. Everything in words that can be exchanged which will heighten your awareness of the reality of her, and her of you, will be multiplied rewardingly in unintelligible ahs of pleasure once you are stroking her body. Your words fly into her mind in the same pulsating way that your penis will penetrate her body. So if with words you can light the eyes in that body; if you can plunge the vaginal recesses of her imagination and bring a twist of anticipation to her lips; or if you pour fluids into that body, alcohol or coffee to stimulate; then without touching her you've made her body a richer delight to partake of and made her more ready and eager for you, for more of you, that is, because you've already been inside her, reaching, caressing.

Learning to talk is not the province of this book. It is assumed that, having the propensity and intelligence to read, you will read and learn and, knowing things, you will have things to say. If there is any guideline beyond that, then it is that there is nothing you can say which is not in your mind, and what is there is peculiar to you as an individual. This is what you must be prepared to give to others in conversation—this part of yourself—and in this matter honesty and candor are of the ultimate merit, irreplace-able. When you talk honestly you are giving of yourself and this practice prepares you and your partner for more giving. The more you give, the more you get.

It follows then, that to project sexuality will be the sum total of your aim in dealings with the opposite sex where you expect to get a return of the same. Projecting sexuality doesn't call for the unsubtle licking of lips, drooling, and standing there playing with your throbbing organ. The art of being sexy and projecting sexuality is a rewarding one, and one much in demand. The key to the vital art is in awareness. Here is one example of vital learning, how to be sexy:

You are sitting across a restaurant table from a desirable woman. You are not talking about similarities between orgasm and the crescendo of a popular concerto, although it might be a good idea under some circumstances, but rather must make your way through the discovery of mutual likes and dislikes, food, entertainment, people, etc. While engaged in this conversation you must make yourself aware that this creature just across the table from you, with her red lips moving around words that select only a small portion of the experience stored in her mind, this creature above all is the possessor of a delicious skin-lined organ to which she is in full control of admissions and which now rests idle on the seat before you, only the scantiest of threads and conventions preventing you from extending your hand at that very minute and reaching inside of her. She pulled on those panties only a short time ago, and can at will remove them for your mutual pleasure.

Against the table, or against her arms, her dress, her brassiere, she is moving two sensitive nipples with every breath she takes, and the air she breathes is the same, from the same cubic yard as you inhale. So that except for a matter of inches and the pace of your breathing, you might now be panting across one another's shoulders, uttering other sounds with less meaning but more sincerity. She's even got her legs drawn up.

Now if you consider this, dwell on it for only an instant during your conversation, you are going to be very much aware of this woman's sexuality, and desirous of sharing, you are going to project a strong sexuality to this woman, who is after all sitting there naked with you, eating you with her mouth and eyes, fondling your private parts with words that caress and agitate and arouse. You will want to touch her, and you will touch her hand or shoulder, and this token will tell her what you want, and one thing will lead to another. Because you are Richard Burton sitting there in your pajamas by candlelight.

To recapitulate, we have seen that it is not important that the male go forth in pursuit of the female only if he possesses a certain arrangement of facial features and a body out of Weightlifters Magazine. What matters is that you be comfortable with yourself and be able to project that comfort, that ease with your body. To gain such comfort, if you do not have it, there is hardly a part of the body that cannot be improved artificially, by care, exercise, or mental adjustment to the conditions which exist.

It is most important that you accept and be at ease with your own body. When you can do that, women will, too.

CHAPTER IV

HOW THE SEXES DIFFER

In barrooms and psychiatric offices all over America, men are asking, "What do women want? Just what the hell do they want in a man?" Of course, the men are asking the question in the wrong room. The answer is in the bedroom. It is inescapable that even the blindest of men must recognize at some point, and the earlier the better, that man possesses at the central point of his physical activity a roughly cylindrical shaped object which extends itself in response to the female, reaching out to fill her, and she–isn't it a coincidence?–harbors within the most protected recess of her body an opening designed for no other purpose than to contain that engorged male cylinder.

To deny this elemental situation is like,

well, trying to start your automobile without inserting a key. A medical associate of mine told me an appropriate joke recently about a rather stoned young person reeling into police headquarters, fumbling with his car keys and asking to make out a stolen car report. "Where was the car the last time you saw it?" asked the desk sergeant, and the youth replied dazedly, "Right here on the end of this key." The sergeant, looking over the disheveled citizen, was not amused; he scolded, "Look at yourself: you're a mess. Your fly is even open." The befuddled youth looked down and exclaimed, "Hey, my girl is gone, too!"

The sensuous male would have to be a bit more aware than that. But the situation is always there, and even when we put it farthest out of our minds, it comes back like the tides. I remember one explicit example of this from my own clinical practice.

One of my patients, an attractive young blonde whose sexuality was such a protruding factor that it was impossible to forget for an instant that here indeed was a female, visited me weekly in my office. Her problem manifested itself in an insatiable appetite for men. She had a lip-licking, earthy quality that practically spelled out sex. She even curled up in her chair in the shape of an "S" and the imagination filled in the rest.

Sometimes a psychologist wonders if he has a moral right to deprive the world of such a creature, but in this case she did have an emotional problem which required treatment. She was a Scandinavian I'll call Ilsa. In our very first session Ilsa described in proud detail her promiscuous activities and announced with considerable conviction, and some alluring leg-crossing, that she wouldn't mind spending our hour in something a bit more physical than psycho-therapy. Well, whatever his private life may be like, and whatever his personal inclinations, there is one thing that no reputable therapist will do and that is to become physically involved with a patient. I put her off for the moment with the suggestion that we had better get to know each other and led the conversation into her problems.

Still, she persisted, that first day and in every subsequent session, taunting a little, declaring, "You know you'd like to–." Of course, any man would have loved to. But that would have been the end of our doctor-patient relationship, so I profusely denied any interest in her body. Each session I had to deny it. But I must have been always aware of it, in spite of what I regarded as my cool professionalism, and she illustrated this to me one day with a laugh. "You know you'd love to," she said, by that point considering the seduction a challenge. "No, no, not at all," I replied calmly, stroking my beard in the best tradition of Freud. "They why," she asked, "is your fly open?"

Needless to say, getting that fly zipped

up, cursing my subconscious, and trying to maintain all the dignity of a detached psychologist guiding his patient was one of those moments in the life of a therapist that fully justifies the high fees we charge. How embarrassing to have our unconscious desires make themselves known despite our efforts to mask them!

The point is, we can relate to females other than sexually, but the basic relationship is always going to be there. If, on the other hand, sex were limited to those basics, to the mere sticking of a penis into a vagina, it would be a dreary world indeed. From a man's point of view, you are obviously attached to that stick; in other words, you come with it. And what you give that panting woman besides a thorough physical penetration is of major consequence.

Females with any degree of maturity know that looks *per se* are no indication of a good lover, and many times can be the reverse. Are you tall, dark and handsome, and well-groomed, impeccably dressed? Well, no woman wants to be shacked up with Frankenstein, but many males who look like they just stepped out of a fashion ad are batting zero. While appearance can be the mark of a considerate person who takes the trouble to look his best, it also can be the mark of self-love to be overly occupied with one's own good looks. Many women fear the too-perfect looker will turn out in the bedroom to be the kind of lover who disrobes and then presents himself with the attitude, "Well, here I am, do me."

The most sought-after traits in a male, according to my personal poll of the most desirable females ever quizzed in the naked, horizontal aftermath, are the qualities of being hip, appearing and acting distinctively, and the capacity for truly appreciating females. Masculinity is not determined by the clothes you have on, but by what you do when you take them off. "Beautiful people" as a term is vague because what really counts is the person's definition of beautiful. To women, a beautiful man is one who is brave enough to be warm, open, kind, considerate, aware, and receptive. The man who is strong enough to be these things, to give that much, will never run out of takers.

Being hip does not require knowing every new expression, every new rock group, or the latest dirty jokes. Hip implies being aware. Aware of yourself, aware of the feelings of others. No one who is open to other humans will ever be very lonesome or very bored. Women who are interested in relationships with men are looking for warm, giving males. This does not apply to material giving but giving of yourself. Warmth in terms of humans is difficult for women to explain. They say they want a "warm" person to go to bed with, and they don't mean just hot-blooded. The phony, insincere men are quickly dropped by wise females before it gets that far.

Warmth in a male often is displayed in touching and caressing, long before entry to the bedroom. Touching seems to be a lost art in our culture. It must be, or people wouldn't find the phenomenon of "sensitivity training" groups so bizarre and intriguing. The sadness is that the sense of touch should be lost in the first place. In Europe the practice of one human touching another when meeting, while talking, in gestures, and in constant closeness, has been preserved to a far greater extent than in America, where the touch often is limited to a perfunctory handshake when meeting, a mere gesture which is immediately denied as being of any significance by a quick withdrawal of one person from another. If you shake the hand of a stranger, the direction to go is closer, if you care. And care you must.

Touching expresses desire, a wish to fondle, to possess. A woman will never resent your desiring to lay her; in fact she loves to excite desire in a man. But nothing turns her off more quickly than the impression that all the man wants is a receptacle for his penis, because this is a fundamental denial that she has anything—tissue, soul, feelings, or anything else—personally attached to that furry sex organ. A woman wants to be given the assurance that it is not just any vagina which will do, but that it must be hers.

After all, she is custodian in full charge

of that sex gate. It is her mind which tells her legs to wrap around your back. It is her feelings that pump her crotch to swallow yours. It is her breasts that urge against your hairy chest and her mouth that abandons the politeness of words to practice gluttony on your lips. She will bring to your love-making her talents, her experience, her eagerness, her softness, and her consideration for your own body's satisfaction, and if you don't want that in addition to the furry little receptacle in her lower torso, then she may well tell you to use your hand instead, or to wander in green pastures where the idea may strike you to sidle up behind a lamb, even furrier, and, they say, not a bad receptacle.

From the moment a woman begins to actively consider the possibility of you as a bed partner, which usually occurs during the intimacy of introduction, she will be examining you to see if you are the male who will be of the school known as the "Wham, bam, thank you ma'am," technique, which is an insult almost as stinging as the slap on the ass that comes with her recognition that any female at all would have done for you. Unless she has been totally, exhaustingly satisfied, the "lover" who climaxes in her then whips it out like a man who has just found himself in the Women's Room by mistake, the man who wordlessly reaches for a cigarette, signalling the end of closeness for the evening, might as well have stuck a knife in her as a penis.

It must be conceded here that some men do have hangups about sex which they cannot overcome overnight. They have been raised to consider the sex act a sort of major or minor crime and begin to feel guilt immediately after performing. Sometimes it is a part of the male personality which, having sacrificed its tendency to hide, having been forced to emerge as a human being in order to establish the minimal relationship necessary for the removal of pants, quickly resents the exposure and slams the door on further closeness the instant the penis shrinks.

Luckily there are enough females with matching or correlative hangups to go around, and we will discuss the diversity of this selection, but the wise male will remember the old adage, only the brave deserve the fair, and in today's world, the man does not demonstrate his bravery by slaughtering buffalo, killing Indians or collecting battle trophies. The bravest man is he who dares to be himself, to expose himself as a human being, without fear. And I'm not talking about those little old men opening their overcoats.

The image of the sensual man has changed vastly through the years. The guy with the over-extended muscles and the physique of a dedicated weight-lifter has become very close to a joke to people who realize that the biggest change in our society today is the reexamination of the relationship between men and women. The 19th century conception of the big, strong, wonderful male to take care of the poor, little, helpless female is happily well on its way out. In past years in my psychological practice it was common to hear males talk about how they were going to "make" this girl or that girl. Today with increasing frequency I hear the female discussing with me how she is going to "make" a certain man.

Some men seem to regard the passing of the so-called virtuous girl of the past with mourning akin to that over the decline in patriotism. For those, there are still plenty of women around with a diversity of hangups over sex that will set their heart a-thumping, but probably in rage.

One patient in particular comes to mind, a married woman in her early twenties named Patricia. She was rather handsome except for her very shy manner. She used a minimum of make-up, dressed drably and hid well what must have been an excellent arrangement of curves. She had very full lips and a face that was generally sensual. Whenever I forgot her name I thought of her as (pardon the expression) "fuck-face" because of what was plainly written there. She was a master, or I should say, mistress, at hiding her feelings. Her problem, as she described it, was the fact that every time she got near men, even strange men, she felt physical desire, often so strong that she would lubricate her panties involuntarily. To suppress this, she had taken to the habit of gazing out the nearest window and preoccupying herself with noting the license numbers of passing cars.

This diversion did the trick. However, so frequent was the incidence or so strong was the desire, that license numbers actually became a passion for her. She would ignore a room full of people to stand at the window and write down the license numbers of cars passing by. The walls of her house became covered with license numbers. Scraps of paper full of license numbers jammed her bureaus and cluttered her shelves and floor. She no longer came in her jeans with such regularity but I was glad to be able to solve her new license obsession. The prescription, oversimplified here, was clear. Rx: Sex, sex, sex, sex, sex.

She has missed an awful lot of license numbers in recent years, but she has made a lot of men very happy, and herself, too. So, if you see a lovely woman writing down license numbers, she may be doing the sexiest thing you ever saw. Think about that.

Or, instead of the sexually liberated woman, perhaps you would rather meet a woman who, like another patient of mine, was only able to indulge in sex by contriving the most outrageous of fantasies. Claire wasn't an outstanding beauty by any means; I gather she tried not to be. She was a little on the thin side and slouched as though trying to obscure the fact that she did possess breasts and other female equipment. She was able to enjoy sex, in fact she was wild about it, and must have been one of the best lays in her congregation. But, in order to permit herself to have sex, she developed the schizophrenic fantasy that she was being seduced each time: It was never her own will, so she was able to forgive herself for participating. But each time, the man seducing her had to be a religious figure. In her fantasy world she had laid a succession of popes and saints that sounded like the history of the church. Now if the right guy came along and tipped his hat and said, "Hello, I'm John the Baptist . . ."

Claire would sit across from me and deny that she had ever experienced sex. She was a virgin, she declared, in fact, *the* Virgin Mary. And although I knew that she personally had taken on the entire night shift of firemen at a certain station, mistaking them for the Twelve Apostles, she *was* right, too, to state that she had never experienced sex. It was not sex to her, not in the fantasy that she created, no matter what it was that the men, one after another, were enjoying. Claire was an extreme case, but she does serve to illustrate the extent to which all humans, and to a great extent women more than men, are subjected to pressures to deny their sensuality.

The moral to the above examples is to rejoice at the sexual liberation of women. If not for your own sake, then for your sons, who are destined to be among the best-laid generation ever to bounce up and down on the face of the earth. It is, after all, rather silly for males, who have spent thousands of years longing to penetrate every attractive girl who ever aimed her cloistered crotch at them, to now resent the idea of females feeling the same way. All those centuries of longing were wasted only because so many of those lusted-after females were not permitted the freedom to long for the same thing. No my darlings, toss your perfumed panties to the wind. Yours is the land of the free, the home of the brave.

The biggest difference between female and male, considering feelings of sexuality, is close to zero in the 1970's. Once her hormones are unrestrained by traditional negative attitudes, we are learning, the woman is every bit as eager a participant in the great love feast as the man. Studies of the use of graphic films and erotic literature indicate that females are equally aroused and in fact, so-called dirty books are enjoying a much greater readership among women than men. Of course, the girls send their men out to buy them, usually, and this is curious.

Usually the girls do not go to erotic bookstores—not out of a lack of daring, but out of delicacy. Watch an attractive girl enter an erotic bookstore and you will see the other customers, all males, that is, hurriedly put down their provocative browsing and as quickly as possible, considering the state of their arousal, slip out of the door. These men feel threatened when a woman penetrates what is considered male territory, because these males have become accustomed to hiding the fact of their sexuality. Such an incident catches them in the act of admitting, almost publically, that they are creatures of desire.

Women are too. The old-fashioned striptease used to give men a chance to observe and appreciate, gradually, the female body and the sexy undergarments worn by women. Today, in the same way that many males are turned on by sexy underwear displayed by women, the girls admit readily that they are turned on by the newer styles of brief shorts and suggestively revealing underwear for men. Given the chance, they are the ones who buy the sexy underwear for their men.

When you do get right down to it—and this, too, is a recommended practice—the principal difference between the sexuality of men and women is in the region specifically delineated at the beginning of this chapter, the physical. A woman is a biologically superior specimen in that her reproductive organs are protectively packaged inside, while a male's dangle perilously at the exterior of the body, vulnerable to attack. In fact, when one considers the placement of the female sex organs, the location, the lining, the encasement within the pelvic bone structure, one realizes that if the heart were indeed the most important organ in the body, it would be placed exactly where the vagina is.

The other basic difference in sexuality is incapacity. Females, in controlled studies with a mechanical superman penis servicing them relentlessly, have been proven capable of experiencing sixty orgasms in an hour. However, they are of varying intensity and usually one huge bell-ringer will bring the female to completion. Males unfortunately are limited to perhaps three or four small ones followed by the big finale. However, for most males and females a single orgasm can suffice. A female also can more easily arouse a male than vice versa, since his genitals are on the outside of his body and can be easily stimulated. The sensual male must learn female anatomy. He must care enough to discover what parts of her body are the points of the greatest excitement to arouse her full expression of sexuality.

It is also interesting in considering differences between male and female to note that only the woman has successfully pursued the role of prostitute, for more obvious reasons than morality. Males cannot become erect on command, while females can fake sex very convincingly. •A man can't fake it. It's either there or it isn't. Try convincing any sexually aware female that you desire her tremendously while having a flaccid penis. Ha!

CHAPTER V

YOUR PENIS AND WHAT TO DO WITH IT

Anybody who urinates standing up should know how to handle the subject matter of this chapter, but unfortunately many do not. This is understandable in view of the scarcity of information regarding man's most vital organ. Even some recent textbooks and so-called sex manuals persist in referring to the penis as the male reproductive organ, which, in and of itself, it is not. It is a sex organ. It is not only functional, it is fun, besides.

Reproduction happens as a byproduct of certain attachments to the penis, but the organ itself is much closer to being man's singular fun organ than his reproductive organ. You have eyes to see with, ears to hear with, a tongue for tasting, a nose for aroma, hands to touch with and a penis for probing inside women. But for our puritan heritage, which chose to apply the terminology for what puritans regarded as the "most noble role" for the penis, the secondary incidence of creating babies, your penis today might well be described in school books as man's sixth sense, for what other organ duplicates its singular sensation?

Until recent years, doctors have been among the dullest and most inept sources of sexual information available—and the most listened to. Even the psychoanalysts, who often tend to regard the erect penis as a weathervane of mental activity, have failed to rise to the occasion successfully. Today, such renowned sex experts as Masters and Johnson admit that when it comes to behavior relating to the crotch, the psychologist is much more savvy.

If the proper study of mankind is man, as the poet says, then this is the proper time to take a good look at the penis. Man is a creature composed along the lines of what is called bilateral symmetry, meaning that in general structure, there are two of almost everything, equally spaced on opposite sides of an imaginary line running from the tip of his nose to the tip of his penis. Two eyes, two nostrils, two lungs, two hips, the legs, the arms—but when it comes to the vital parts, the brain, the heart and the penis, there is only one of each. When you consider that the singularity of the other vital organs, such as the heart and head, is mitigated to some extent, the heart invisibly hidden in the interior and the head divided by eyes and eyebrows, cheeks, clefts in chin and lips, and the line of the nose, one must admit that the penis is indeed an extraordinary part of the man, standing alone, and is intended to play a key position in his life.

So much for anatomy. From a certain point of view, the penis is the great equalizer of mankind. All men are *not* born equal, except, in most cases, by their anatomy. But in the same way that they called the six shooter the Great Equalizer in the Old West, there were some more equal than others, depending on their skill in using that particular implement.

Just a short time ago I was invited to visit the regular Friday night meeting of a Hollywood sex club. It was the kind of club that stressed socializing, where couples would meet and talk before pairing off from the living room and departing to the privacy of bedrooms. In the living room were a friendly group of some half dozen men and an equal number of women. All were making conversation, trying to capture the fascination of one girl or another.

It was irritating to notice, however, that several of the girls, one at a time, were getting up and walking down the hallway, pausing at a doorway across from the bathroom, leaning there as though they were listening to a great symphony rather than just waiting to get into the bathroom. And when they came back, their eyes still drifted toward that door. One girl would whisper to another and off the other girl would go.

I finally decided I had to find out what the big attraction was in the hallway, so I excused myself on the same pretext of going to the bathroom. At the doorway next to the bedroom, the door was slightly ajar, to a bedroom there, pitch black inside. Inside, however, you could distinctly hear the sounds of a woman in the most exquisite passion. I have never heard such a succession of oh, oh, oh, Oh, OH!, ohhhh, oooohhh, every possible variation of oh. That's what was capturing the fascination of all the other girls. And they couldn't keep their eyes off the doorway because they wanted to be sure to see who the *guy* was that came out.

When he finally emerged, and hardly a girl budged until he did, there was no outburst of applause. But with all the advertising that his partner had done for him with her own moans of pleasure, that guy, who was not a particularly outstanding man in appearance, nor a greatly expressive one vocally, could have had any girl in the house by crooking his finger at her, whether his penis hung as flaccid as a waterlogged rope or as rigid and soaring as a telephone pole.

The moral to the story is that it's not

what you have, but how you use it. Probably no myth in the whole realm of sexuality has been as widespread and tenacious as the fallacy that some men are hung enormously larger than others and that women will always crave the giant and shun the smaller. The truth about the relative size of the penis from man to man is that it is a factor of negligible importance. Women are the first to confirm this. Those who have tried what looked like an enormous penis that could penetrate them up to the chest cavity, and who have also tried a ho-hum looking, pencil-size one (before insertion), have almost unanimously voted for the penis that does the most for them, and this is seldom the biggest.

The biggest penis may be that which just happens to be in the state of fullest engorgement, meaning that it is closest to coming. The quick comer turns off girls, who do not like to be left panting and unfulfilled, and more often then not, that big huge penis is reduced to a weak, wet, limp string in seconds. The man who can control his penis has the key to a girl's heart.

In terms of size, there are some penises which look larger than others in the idle, unstimulated state. But at the peak of excitement, the difference in size of penis from a six-foot-two football player to that of a five-foot-seven clerk is minimal. Men have always had some kind of hangup about this situation. This has been a major factor in relations with the Negro race, and I use the expression fully aware of the equivocation.

The myth that Negroes all have enormous penises and that if interracial love is allowed then the Negroes will woo away all the most beautiful white girls, grew to such a currency because masculine self-confidence is at such a low ebb. Of course, most insecure whites said it was the white *jobs* that the Negroes would take away if they weren't kept in place, because men do not like to raise the question of their own possible sexual insecurity. Which also is one of the basic reasons a man insists on marriage and faithfulness of his wife. His ego could not stand the possibility that his wife might convulse in sexual glee under the body of another man.

But we are drifting away from the subject. Size is of little importance. A girl can insert enormous objects into her vagina. When she is fully aroused, properly moistened and gradually penetrated, she can accept a rounded cylinder three inches in diameter and sometimes up to ten inches long. Tests of this amazing capacity have actually been made in the laboratory with dozens of willing women volunteers.

They were laid out naked on a padded laboratory table, with a camera grinding away at them and their crotches. A mechanical penis was used, rigged on a brace that swung automatically in the same angle of a man's penetration if she were being laid in the traditional or missionary position. The soft plastic penis itself was adjustable. A screw mechanism inside it, like a vise, permitted the instrument to be gradually enlarged, and the girl could control this enlargement herself by remote control, through a hookup at the back, unpenetrating end of the penis, or in this case, dildo.

It was a great opportunity for girls to experiment with what it would feel like to have an enormous penis, with no limitations on its endurance, plunging into them unto satiation. Most of these volunteers (in the name of science, of course) optioned to gradually swell the dildo to its maximum at some stage of the game, which is a salutary comment on the mental health of women and their willingness to experiment, or to enjoy sex, whichever way you regard the matter. Well, it was a great thrill, of course, but most of them commented on some discomfort in being repeatedly prodded by the larger imitation organ, without that much additional satisfaction.

Actually, when you consider that a thing the size of a ten-pound baby can make its way out of that amazing cave, its big round head first, and that this can be done naturally, without sedation, it's no wonder that such large imitation male organs can be inserted in there. On the other hand, the vagina, in its state of excitement, not only has the capability of enlargement to accept whatever wishes to enter, it also naturally contracts, so that if you were sliding a ball-point pen in and out, the sides of the vagina would grip the instrument, flex on it tightly at every thrust, and it would be every bit as full as it was in the case of the three-inch dildo.

If you don't believe it, ask your girl to try an experiment with you. Make love to her or tease her until she is hot to the point of reception. Actually, licking her clitoris with your tongue would bring about the optimum state. Laboratory machines such as those described above are hard to build, but they'd probably sell, if someone manufactured them. So, instead, you will have prepared two objects for the experiment. One is a normal-size vibrator, the kind which is made in the shape of a penis, with a rounded tip and self-contained battery power safely contained within. The other is your selection of the largest dildo you can find, or, since most sales outlets categorize them by size, one about two-and-a-half inches in diameter and nine inches long. Since dildoes are expensive—even though every house might use one—and since this may be a one-time experiment, a cucumber may be substituted for either the smaller or larger instrument, or both. Don't shop for cucumbers with a tape measure, however, unless you're willing to be subjected to considerable giggling from the salesgirls.

Both instruments, vegetable or plastic, should be placed in a lubricated prophylactic, or rubber, because this is more tender on the delicate tissue of the female interior. When you have licked or otherwise stimulated your girl to the point where she is panting for penetration, gently ease your finger into her, stir softly but thoroughly, and then begin to insert the *larger* of the two instruments first. Play the nose of the dildo around her wet clitoral area, dip it into the vagina and retract it with the measured thrusts of an enjoyable sexual intercourse. With each stroke, bury it further, until her body has accommodated the entire thing, or as much as she can take. Most girls, unless they are inexperienced, virginal, restricted by fear of pain or sexual tension, or otherwise undilated, will be able to take almost the full size. However, it will not be too comfortable and will not glide in and out with ease. The withdrawal stroke is likely to please her more than the penetration. The very idea of bigness may excite her at first, she too being a victim of the myth of magic in the penis of a giant, but soon the discomfort of it will overcome the unusualness of the situation.

At this point, lay the large instrument aside and begin teasing her with the smaller one, again playing at the clitoral area and teasing at the lips of her vagina. When you begin gradual strokes with the smaller penis substitute, her greatly expanded vagina will contract and fit around it every bit as tightly as with the larger one, and full in-and-out motions will be more pleasurable because they are softer and permit her the latitude of moving herself to greet the penetration, a situation which is fraught with difficulty with the bulky king-size rubber penis. Actually, the pressure of the larger instrument, which concentrates her sex organ muscles into expanding laterally, gives less pleasure because the lateral expansion reduces the longing for swifter, deeper thrusts.

The issue should be obvious. That is, take a look at the larger one. How would you like to have it penetrate you? It should be mentioned in passing that such an experiment on your girl is not a bad idea for giving her the best lay she has ever had. If you have already come once with her, then by the time you have finished your experiment you will be ready to go again, and when she gets a warm, alive male in her after all that stimulation, it will be most satisfying, for both of you.

One final word before dispensing—forever, I hope—with the notion that penis size is a cause for anxiety in the male and lust in the female. I had a female patient once named Martha, who came from the Midwest. In fact, she had lived on a small ranch before moving to the city with her husband. Her marriage was stormy at first, because she made extraordinary sexual demands upon her husband. She was the kind of woman who would not have to be asked to participate in such an experiment as described above. She would come home with the cucumbers and suggest it herself.

With this kind of a powerful sex drive, and a husband willing to accommodate her, one would think their marriage would be ideal. Not so. Martha—and by the way, she was the freckle-faced kind of girl-next-door type who you would think got more of a kick singing in the church choir or playing volleyball than from sex—was insatiable. Her husband could bring her to orgasm three times in a night and she would work on him with every trick of lip and thigh to get it up again for another go, even if it took till dawn.

Needless to say, the problem became just as much the husband's, who was losing weight and showing up at work in the mornings looking as though he'd spent the whole night working out, which often was the case. But after the husband had tried everything in the book to satisfy Martha, everything she could think of, and she was a very imaginative girl sexually, his enthusiasm began to wane. This is natural on his part, because the male sexual drive relies to a certain extent on the satisfaction of seeing his woman satisfied. If he finds himself capable of extraordinary performances in number and endurance, it may bring a smile to his face, but if at the end of it all his wife is not smiling, too, then he starts to feel that there must be something wrong with him, his technique, his penis, or something.

Martha finally had come to fantasize a solution to her problem. She grabbed hold of an idle inspiration from her youth and clung to it tenaciously. The fantasy was this: she believed that if she could once, just once in her life be "serviced" by a stallion, she would be completely satisfied.

Oversimplified, it was penis size she sought—the biggest possible. Of course, in her early life on a ranch she had witnessed the common sight of a stud mounting a mare with that incredible red instrument. Well, Martha longed to be laid by a horse. My experience with veterinarian consultants is limited, but as an observer who is no stranger to country life I would guess that the penis of a full-size stallion measures about five inches in diameter and could have reached up to her mouth, if it could ever get in.

Martha was nonetheless a very strong-minded girl, particularly when it came to fulfillment of her sexual desires, and despite my efforts to quickly brush aside this fantasy as certainly not being the answer to her problems, Martha was determined that she would try it. She even went to the extent of figuring out a way to overcome the obvious objection to equine sex partners, the fact that the animal's weight would crush a normal person in the process. She figured that if a harness hoist of the type used by horse doctors to keep an animal's weight off an injured leg could be employed around the front end of a docile horse's body, it would solve the weight problem. She also had decided that she would need a sturdy bench, with a deep mattress to give herself plenty of cushioning, or leeway, but she hadn't decided how high the bench should be, and this one point she even asked my advice about. She said that she could see the hoist and halter working efficiently to raise the horse's front end, and that she could slide under the animal, wash its worthy sex organs and toy with them to stimulate an erection (and I suspected that she had actually carried out the part of trying to masturbate a horse to bring it to erection), but the problem of the height of the bench was a big stumbling block to her.

Since she only wanted to do this once, she said she wanted everything right the first time. Really, she enjoyed discussing it so much I think she came thinking about it. What she actually asked me, by way of assisting in her experiment, was that since the height of the bench depended on it, did she think that she would have to settle for rear entry, on her hands and knees, or could she be on her back to lay the steed?

Now, you will never meet a girl more hung up on penis size than that one, but do you know what Martha's problem really was? She had a long-standing terror of homosexuality—her own. She had within herself unresolved lesbian tendencies. Everybody has within themselves to some extent a homosexual component that is retained from the process of growing up, but with some people it is stronger than others, and if it is not accepted, if it terrifies the person, then he or she tends to overcompensate for it. Thus Martha's drive was her way of acting out the super-female. In other words, a girl who had such a strong sex drive couldn't possibly have anything of a lesbian inclination, not when she was the ultimate in females, who had even had intercourse with a horse!

This was her way of denying something she could not face. I tried very hard to get her to accept the harmless fact that there was a trace of homosexuality in her (as there is in all of us at some time or another, usually never acted upon), but it took over a year of therapy, and, meanwhile, her husband gave up on her. All during that year she spent a good deal of time going to the races, and not auto races. She studied each entry with high-powered binoculars. I don't know if she ever did find a set of circumstances, a man to help, and the other conditions which would have made it possible for her to fulfill her fantasy of the ultimate penis.

After she quit therapy I met her years later. I didn't want to bring up the subject and she never said. It may have been passing up a comment for the medical history books, but I suspected that if she had actually contrived to do it (and I wouldn't be surprised if someone has) she would be too sore to talk about it. Sore in the crotch for one thing. Doubly sore because, from what veterinarians tell me, a stallion is actually a pretty lousy lay. They climb on, shove it in, and it only takes two or three thrusts before they spill their semen—about a bucket full.

It is possible, by the way, for females of one species to attract species of another, and to even make them come. As a matter of fact, one very successful female animal trainer employed this system. She never carried a whip. What she did do was to go to the animals' cages before her act and jerk them all off, tigers and lions. When they got into the ring with her before the crowd, they were so grateful they would just sit there and purr contentedly at her, and they'd do anything she suggested. Large animals are very much attracted to the human female—even though, since the average tiger weighs about four or five hundred pounds and has claws and teeth that get mighty playful when the animal is excited, I doubt if you'll ever meet a girl who wants to lay a tiger, a real one. Any male who wishes to attempt the ultimate real lady tiger is welcome to try, but remember, tigers may not accept substitutes.

I should make it clear that intercourse with any other animals except human females is not advocated by this book and the aforementioned tales are a matter of sexual lore. No, the human female has between her legs, and between her lips, and her other contrivances for enclosure, everything that your penis requires.

Still, in the absence of suitable females, it is astounding the things a man will stick his penis into for pleasure. One such example will serve to illustrate a basic part of the *modus operandi* of the penis that is a valuable piece of information.

When I was serving an internship at a hospital years ago—a big city hospital—a man came into the emergency room in the dead of night with a very embarrassing problem manifested by an unusual bulge in his pants. His problem: his penis was stuck in a length of pipe. It's not that unusual; men stick their sex organ into milk bottles, knotholes, flashlights, any receptacle you can imagine.

In this case, the man had taken the caution of lining the interior of the pipe with melted wax. He probably was engaged in the masculine equivalent of the female's horse fantasy, that of entering an exceedingly tight virgin. It may be completely aside from the point, but laying very tight virgins is usually a bore in reality. Not only do you get an extremely bruised foreskin and over-all scraped penis, but if it is that tight, then the girl doesn't enjoy it and female enjoyment is almost a *sine qua non*—a necessity—for the complete enjoyment of the male.

But what happened to this man's fantasy was that it was too good. While in his imagination he was penetrating a virgin who writhed in discomfort at having seven inches of pulsating bone shoved inside her for the first time, his penis was getting larger and larger, filling the pipe. The enlargement of the penis is a matter of stimulation of the nerves which travel from the brain to the groin, attaching to the penis at about the juncture of the rectum. Imagination, friction, or other stimulation sends an extraordinary amount of blood to the penis area, and the vessels of the penis are unique in their ability to retain this blood, soaking it up. The rush of blood, filling the muscle and tissue of the penis, is what causes its enlargement, which is why it is at its largest just before coming—that is the instant when the most blood is activated. The semen squirts out under pressure of throbbing blood, and when this fluid is ejected, the blood is able to drain back out, relaxing the penis.

However, when thrust into a pipe with an active imagination and considerable friction working for it, there is too much pain to come and too much friction for the blood to cease being agitated, so the blood stays, the erection stays, and the man panics and can't withdraw. In this case, a hacksaw had to be applied to the pipe to cut it off, and if you can imagine the tight fit, his penis was a bit sore by the time the "surgery" was done.

Never forget that the object is enjoyment, fun. Meanwhile, this chapter should assure you once and for all that being male—unless you have experienced some traumatic incident such as surgical amputation or a near-fatal loss at swordplay—you possess as mighty an organ as is required to do the job. There is no need to fear comparisons in size. Technique is far more important, anyway. For explicit instructions in getting the most out of your sex organ, which is a muscle and needs exercising, read on.

CHAPTER VI

CREATIVE MASTURBATION

If you are going to masturbate, and sometimes it is recommended, then it is perhaps best to stick with your hand. The variability of pressures that can be applied by the fist and fingers is capable of giving a complete range of feelings. There is absolutely nothing wrong with masturbation. Generations of children grew up masturbating in the face of dire warnings that warts or yellow stains would appear on their hands, or hair would grow there, marking them forever as despicable masturbators. Even doctors of a generation ago believed that masturbation in excess could cause insanity. All of this is of course nonsense—moral distortions that stem from our puritanical heritage. If you are without women and do not masturbate, the body takes care of it for you, spilling your semen out at night amidst some dream of sexual delight. Why not be awake and enjoy the pleasure while relieving yourself?

If periodic or regular masturbation is required to fill the gaps in your sexual life, don't be ashamed of it. Masturbation won't hurt anybody, but shame will. It is a perfectly healthy exploitation of a bodily capability for pleasure. As a matter of fact there are devices on the market—buy the sex magazines and you'll see the ads—such as an artificial vagina and a hot water attachment that practically sucks you off in the bathtub, and while these are not preferable to the female or the fist, the reason is not a condemnation of the devices. It's simply that using the devices, procuring them and coming to rely on them, tends to replace the female as the goal of sexuality, and this is a stunting of sexual growth. The artificial vagina, a plastic, skin-colored contraption, actually is designed to be worn by one person while another inserts his penis, thus the device is largely used by homosexuals. The water masturbator is used for solo performances, but again, man should not be permanently restricted to a solitary sex life.

Ideally, masturbation should be performed as a means of stimulating and improving sexual performance with females. There is considerable difference between male and female masturbation, the difference arising out of the fact that the organs are of different capabilities. Doctors and psychiatrists who are modern-minded are advising young women who have difficulty in reaching orgasm with their husbands to masturbate. When the woman is controlling the touch of her own organs, she can bring on the maximum orgasm, and can do it often. Rather than draining her sexually, masturbation actually makes her sexier; it stimulates her sexuality, makes her more conscious of the pervading power of that thing in her loins, and if she can rid herself mentally of hangups about masturbating, it increases the possibility that she can also get over whatever hangups she may have about "committing" the sex act with a male.

There are two principles to be considered when approaching masturbation as an adjunct to, or betterment of the male performance. First of all, the major part of masturbation is not really the manipulation of the foreskin back and forth over the glans knob in a pleasurable manner; it is what goes on in fantasy.

A man sees a gorgeous body in mini-skirt from his window and retires to the bathroom to relieve the sudden excitement. Memory and imagination come into play, to add to the pleasure of self-touch. While memory is important in sparking the initial desire, imagination is the key factor determining just how good it is going to be. I would suggest that you direct this imagination into creating the girl of your dreams, so that when it does come to pass, you will have helped your sex life by playing with yourself rather than possibly cluttered it with difficulty by creating impossible situations.

Think of a girl with a specific set of features—the color of hair, the face, the lips, the shape of her body, and touch your organ the way you would have yourself feel in the process of warming her up and penetrating her. If you gently prod the end of your penis with a moist fingertip the way her tongue might initiate the process of sucking you, you are fantasizing about a real desire. If you just slide a hand openly along the side of your penis, the way it might rub against her leg while you are preparing her, you are learning delay, learning to give, which is the best possible sexual learning.

Don't create a rigid set of circumstances and repeat it time after time with every masturbation. Vary the girl you create so that you can accept a variety of women, no matter who it is you will later find yourself mated with, no matter what she looks like nor what her specific desires may be. Do not confine your fantasies to your own pleasure while stroking your organ; learn to derive the greater part of your pleasure from the administering of pleasure to your fantasy girl. There will come a time when this girl will be beside you, and what you give to her by way of real sexual thrills will be a major factor in deciding whether or not she, in turn, will be inspired to deliver you to the heights of ecstasy.

There is nothing wrong with fantasizing, as long as we do not let it replace reality. Always let your fantasies work toward reality. You will never fulfill yourself as a sensuous male in your bathroom or solitary bed, but you can save your fantasies and one day, maybe tomorrow, or maybe in a half hour, there will be—you *must* find her—there *will* be a girl and, if she fits the pattern of the dream girl you have been copulating with your hands, you might be able to say to her, after the initial experience, "You know, I have a fantasy about sex in which the woman and I are naked in bed and—"

She may be eager to share it with you, make it come true, and, then, tell you *her* fantasies, so that you can perform for her. In this way, masturbation is headed in the direction of sexual fulfillment rather than replacing it.

Unlike women, however, a man cannot in the usual circumstances just finish orgasm and then make it with a girl. A girl may lie abed, toying with her moist clitoris until she comes repeatedly, a dozen times; she can even stimulate herself into semi-conscious rapture, and then still take on a lover the minute she pulls her hand out. A man spills his semen and then, if suddenly the girl he has been dreaming about knocks at the door stark naked, he is standing there with a useless instrument in his hand.

Which brings us to masturbation as a means of controlling ejaculation. Since controlled ejaculation—the ability to remain hard for a long period while driving the girl wild with delight—is the key to being a sexually competent lover, masturbation, practiced with care, can be a useful method of prolonging the sexual experience. The problem and complication of premature ejaculation will be covered in a later chapter, but to the extent that early ejaculation can be every male's problem it is considered here.

If, for example, you are in a situation with a woman with whom you are only able to be intimate on weekends, or twice a week, you face a problem that the first time you make it with her after an absence, your testicles are ready to send you spurting the instant you enter her. Masturbation could help if, in preparation for your intimacies, you relieved yourself. Not only do you enter the bedroom with an ardor heightened by your self-manipulation, but you have the added factors going for you of (1) since you have just had a sexual experience, you are able to reach for greater heights of sensuality, and (2) since you have ejaculated, the pressure to relieve your love-making system is not going to be overwhelming.

However, the big danger here is timing. If you are in robust good health, full of vitamins and not lacking in energy or sleep, then you could masturbate within a half hour of performing with your girl. On the other hand, while anticipation of the things you are going to do together may arouse you and make masturbation seem like a great idea, if you are not in good shape you may be deluding yourself. You may masturbate and then find yourself either unable to perform with your partner or worse, uninterested in doing it. One must learn one's own capacity in this and not let sudden urges prompt masturbation when it might be a big mistake in timing. You've got to leave yourself time to recover fully and it is better to pass up masturbating altogether than spoil a love-making session by trying to make it better.

There are at least six other methods of extending the length of time your penis is inside your partner, which prolongs the enjoyment for both of you. Most of these methods require some practice to perfect, but, as we indicated early in this chapter, the man who controls his penis is a man much in demand.

First, it is possible to learn to ejaculate only small amounts of semen at a time. This requires considerable control, since the male cannot let himself and his passions run free, shooting for the maximum orgasm. You tease the woman's clitoris with the tip of your penis, stroke into her gently, and when the stimulation reaches its first peak, do not hold off for the big bang, but let a little go. Then, after a pause during which you suck a nipple and maintain stimulation upon her without heightening your own explodability, you continue, reach another little peak and let another small emission go.

One trick in retaining hardness without fully ejaculating is to stroke with your groin, so that you are rubbing against her most sensitive part, the clitoral area, with the juncture of your penis and your body. You are still penetrating her fully but you are eliminating the push-pull movement that would cause you to spill yourself; also, you are allowing your penis to relax and recover a moment while diverting your stimulation of her to another area, not once discontinuing it. With practice, not only will you be able to continue for as long as four times the average "inside" time, arousing her to fullest passion, but by interrupting your own progress, you will bring off a bigger orgasm for yourself than otherwise possible, when you finally do let go. She'll love you for it.

There is a physical aid which should be mentioned in passing, and that is to refrain from urinating before the sexual act. If the bladder contains some fluid, a set of life-long trained muscles unconsciously operates to restrict the ejection of fluid, and, meanwhile, the pressure of the partially swollen bladder exerts a constricting action on the seminal duct through which semen must pass for ejaculation.

On the other hand, or we should say at

the other end, it is a good idea to relieve the bowels well before sexual foreplay. The nerves which run from the brain to the penis are channeled through the rectal area, and any pressure inside the rectum is a stimulation which the brain may interpret as sexual and therefore can prompt overexcitement which explodes the climax abruptly and forcefully. If you don't believe this, have your girl stick her finger into your anus before you ejaculate. The thrill will keep you spurting semen until there's not a drop left in you.

Knowledgeable courtesans of long ago used to make use of these factors. One such practice began with the man taking an enema to empty and purify the rectum. The courtesan—which is a fancy word for a whore of the top-notch professional variety—had a strand prepared which consisted of silky, thin string, knotted at intervals. During the process of laying her man, she would gradually push this strand, knot by knot, at the end of a finger into his rectum, ideally filling it by the time he was reaching his climax. The instant he started to come, she would pull the end of the string, which she kept rolled around her index finger, jerking it out of the anus in one swift but gentle movement, each knot stimulating as it exits, and the man, exploding from two different directions, shoots off as he has never done before.

But the rectal trick is not one for delaying orgasm but heightening it. Probably the best known and most used method of attempting to delay orgasm is to concentrate on the female's desires, not your own. If the female comes first, and she's a sensual girl, she is not going to deny you your orgasm, so there's no reason why you shouldn't delay entry until the last possible moment, and even then, keep your head about you enough to do what the female would want.

There should not be an idle part of your body. Your hands should be busy caressing her, your lips should be kissing her, your eyes watching her, your tongue teasing her and saying things to her between kisses, and if you have all these different pursuits to engage in, you are not going to be concentrating all your consciousness on the single organ, your penis, which will explode too quickly if you do. Some manuals recommend turning your thoughts to other things, like entertaining a fantasy about an asexual skiing trip in the cold, cold snow, or listening to noises outside the room and imagining what other people are doing. But this is the exact opposite of what sex is all about. Sex is involvement. If you absolutely can't delay orgasm without turning off your sensory delight in what you're doing, perhaps it is best to turn your thoughts away, but this is the least desirable method. After all, if you are going to employ a mental valve of this sort, you could start thinking about the pressure of overdue bills, summon up fears about highway accidents, or evoke the ghost of whatever it is that gets you most uptight. And if you do, swift ejaculation may indeed cease to be your problem; in fact, you may end up within a few minutes with the inability to maintain an erection at all. Sex is sex. Dilute it as little as possible, like good wine.

Amphetamines are another method of prolonging erection without ejaculation, but since use of these pills is restricted almost everywhere to prescription, you'd have to have a very understanding doctor to employ this method. (Amphetamines are used both for diet control and to offset depression. There *is* the argument that you tend to get depressed about coming too quickly, and sexual athletics are a great means of reducing!) On the other hand, if you do have a prescription, sex while influenced by amphetamines can be very interesting. Some men can go on for an hour that way, staying hard all along. Only trouble is, with some men, they can keep going, but they can't come; it's a drug and that's sometimes the way it affects a person.

Needless to say, no such stimulants—in the drug subculture amphetamines are known as "uppers"—should be taken without consulting a physician since they act on vital bodily processes. Marijuana is another stimulant that has found considerable favor with some love-makers, who claim that it not only prolongs, but intensifies every instant of the sexual experience. But here again, unless you live in a country where marijuana is legal, a careful respect of the law is in order. After all, for one fantastic, pot-abetted orgasm—no matter what heights are reached—you are risking being placed in a cell deprived of women for years.

Finally, another method gaining some popularity among compassionate, well-adapted young couples is this: the male of course takes his time about initial entry, but when he gets in he makes his strides full and meaningful until the point at which he feels he is about to come. Abruptly he withdraws. The woman, knowing the meaning of the withdrawal as a signal, reaches down and grabs his penis, catching the ridge of the glans penis (the edge of the red knob where it meets the skin section) between her thumb and forefinger and squeezing hard enough to close the passage inside.

Physically, this pressure sends a message back that the duct is closed and ejaculation hesitates, while the squeezing is a distinctly enough separate action from screwing, and painful enough, that it does stall the process temporarily. The motion can be repeated several times; or the man can do it to himself. However, for psychological reasons, it is better for the woman to do it. It spreads the partnership feeling for one thing, even though it may be difficult to understand how having a woman seize your penis is going to be an interference with orgasm. If it's left to the male to do, he is liable not to squeeze hard enough. Being in the state of near orgasm, he is probably reluctant to forestall such a great feeling. The female partner is capable of applying the required pressure more objectively. Besides, wouldn't you rather have her do it?

Before proceeding to describe your other tools of sex and how to use them, one final word about your sex organ. For years it was argued that circumcised persons were able to last inside a woman much longer than uncircumcised men. Since, in the former case, the raw, sensitive head of the penis had been exposed to a good deal of rubbing, it was presumed to be less sensitive and slower to react.

This factor, however, is offset by the circumcision itself, which exerts a kind of pressure more directly on the delicate meaty part during vaginal friction. The uncircumcised, who do exercise their penis by drawing the foreskin back and forth from time to time, if only for sanitary purposes, are compensated in intercourse by having that foreskin as a sort of sexual shock absorber, and thus, it all comes out even.

Recognizing then, that your penis is physically a muscle and that there should be no shame attached to exercising it—you may learn by practice to flex it but it will never expand like biceps—you may enjoy masturbation as often as you wish, secure in the knowledge that regular use will only benefit your sexuality. On the other hand, the use of fantasy can heighten your prowess in man-woman sexual expression, and there are many methods to employ to delay the ultimate reaction of your penis, the orgasm, thereby enhancing the enjoyable moments leading up to it.

CHAPTER VII

LOVE, THE BEST APHRODISIAC

Plato in *The Apology* paraphrases Socrates when he says, "The unexamined life is not worth living." This profound thought from the ancient Greeks has been carried down through the ages and today is the rationale for much psychology and psychiatry. To examine life and not probe every fine detail of sensual behavior would be to overlook the deepest and innermost needs of humans, and the expression of them.

When historians look back on the current era, the last third of the twentieth century, they will probably note the emergence of a new freedom of the spirit and a prevalence of stress upon feeling. Live, live, live, cry the trend-setters. Try any new experience, sample everything, leave no sensation unexplored; and concommitantly, anything which springs uncluttered from instinct, smacks of innocence, or even explodes the personality to its limits is deemed desirable.

Sooner or later this trend, which is long overdue and fosters the best in human capacity, will nevertheless have to be tempered with thought and examination, and will be the better for it. The most casual observer of the human scene can find overwhelming evidence that everyone is interested in sensuality. As outmoded as introspection may be on the current psychological scene, all of us indulge in self-examination, and this is all for the good if we can do it liberated from the hangups that permit us to deceive ourselves. For we are always held within the walls of ourselves no matter what we do.

The practice of administering pleasure to another human as a means of satisfying our own deepest physical longings is one of the few ways open to man for escaping the walls of self. The wisdom of this anatomical destiny as a preconceived plan for forcing man to communicate and share, while simultaneously spreading good feeling, may be perhaps the single most outstanding facet of involuntary human nobility.

That may sound almost biblical in inspiration, and indeed at times the entire area of sensuality may seem to be best approached from a simple, old-fashioned, common sense point of view. However, one soon finds that common sense may indeed be common or general, but its sense is surrounded by prejudice, superstition, and acres of wishful thinking.

For example, the popular idea that love will conquer all is a myth. The nature of romantic love as a psychological vacuum, a magnetic pull toward fulfilling a person's own estimated shortcomings, is a well-known phenomenon discussed elsewhere. It will suffice here to point out that even though you may love another person with every fiber of your body, your love cannot repair a broken leg or a psychotic breakdown.

Let me illustrate what I consider to be the highest contribution of love to the development of human sensuality with a narration of a non-clinical experience which was told to me by an acquaintance concerning a girl he had met at a party. He didn't know at the time that the young woman—I'll call her Julia—was currently a patient of mine.

Given Julia's particular problem, which will be made clear as you read on, I took pains to extract from my acquaintance the most minute details regarding Julia's behavior while she was with him. He was happy to cooperate in recalling what was for him an unforgettable experience.

Henry met my patient—an attractive young blonde—at a party with a liberated young group of people. But Julia seemed to be a wallflower. Despite an alluring set of facial characteristics, highlighted by a pert, bobbed nose and an expression of casual detachment, she sat alone in a corner, her legs curled under her shapely body. Apparently she had already repelled several attempts by others to strike up a conversation with her. She seemed to resent the openness, the liberal attitudes of most of the crowd, along with their free attitudes about sex.

With considerable difficulty, my enterprising friend took the challenge and managed to engage Julia in conversation. Henry's guess was right; she was firm-lipped in her opposition to the way most of the people at this particular party carried on, their talk and their actions. The question was, why did she come here? She *was* open-minded enough to discuss it, however, and with his practiced manner of encouraging such expression Henry got Julia to talk about her feelings. She did not believe in making love to comparative strangers. Never. How animalistic! She did not believe in oral love-making. She frowned on the so-called French arts, the Greek arts. *She* did not want strange lips on her breasts. Not *her.*

Later (it was an hour later, only one drink later, but a few thousand words later) they agreed to go to a bedroom to continue their talk in an atmosphere of privacy, the crowd around them having begun to interrupt a bit boisterously. No sooner were they inside the quiet, softly-lit bedroom than she declared out of a clear blue, "I love you!"

With no further ado she unzipped the side of her powder blue micro-miniskirt, shunted her flaring hips twice, bump, bump, in a practiced motion that let the garment fall free to the carpet. She continued to strip, peeling off her panty-hose and even her panties while Henry stretched out on the bed in utter fascination at the change in her. When her panties hit her ankles, she stepped out of one side and, with the other foot, twirled the dainty garment twice in a circle like a sling before letting it fly with such carefree abandon that he too began to remove his clothing.

Hoisting her turtleneck jersey over her head, she pulled bra and all with it, and at that instant, standing there in splendid beauty and nakedness, my patient made a characteristic gesture that was so graceful and appealing that it commanded love of the most tender variety. It was a kind of one-handed, limp-wrist flip, discarding the remainder of her clothes the way a magician snaps his fingers and creates a puff of smoke. She had made one Julia disappear. This was the other Julia.

Henry was ready for her, a bit astounded, however, and still cognizant of the specific limitations she placed on the physical expression of love. They embraced and he found her body lovely, her breasts a trifle small considering the wicked curve of her hips, but firm and with nipples erect. Her crotch, and she really was a blonde, was already moist, but Henry intended to delay entering her; he wanted to be especially gentle, considering her earlier protestations of purity.

Before he could take the initiative, however, she mounted *him,* sliding her voluptuous weight down on his penis with the sigh of a satisfied person lowering her body into the most comfortable chair in the house. She proceeded to move in a practiced and highly stimulating fashion. She had wonderful control of the muscles in her vagina, and while she moved she gripped his penis with an expert inner tension. She bent carefully forward and dangled the tips of her breasts, one by one, into his mouth, letting him catch them. When Henry sucked her nipples she went wild, letting her hips churn and twist and press and practically fly in a whole new series of motions that made him feel like he was screwing something between a human washing machine and an aircraft preparing for takeoff.

There are moments when no delaying tactics are going to forestall orgasm, and this lovely creature's body brought him to the edge of climax so swiftly he couldn't believe it. She grunted with every slap of her lower torso against his; he knew she, too, was ready to go. He bit her nipple gently and with a shuddering movement and scream she climaxed as he did.

It was lovely, Henry said. He loved Julia

at that moment, and stared at her, still a bit dazed at the almost schizophrenic change in her from fifteen minutes ago. She lay silently next to him with her head on his chest, and he could see that she had no intention of getting up. Even though they had only been in the room for minutes, their frenzy had practically soaked a section of the sheets. Julia did not appear inclined to move to a dry spot. In fact, she savored it, the odor of love that filled the room, and her nostrils flared as she rested her face on his sweaty chest. She spoke differently, too. "It was great, wasn't it," she said. Henry replied, "Yes, *you* were great. Your body is wonderful, and the way you use it is magnificent."

As she spoke she reached down and caressed his penis and testicles with her fingers, enjoying the wetness of them, a wetness that had come from her. She kissed him and ran her tongue down his chest, across his nipples and navel. She rolled the tip of her tongue delicately against his testicles, and licked into the recesses of his thighs. She knelt down on her own ankles, her head buried in his crotch, and lifted his testicles tenderly to the crevices of her breasts and held them there. She ran her tongue around the tip and rim of his penis and then slid her lips over the red tip, moving back and forth just on the tip. In a matter of seconds her exquisitely shaped ass was up in the air and her mouth descended on his penis to the full length.

Henry glanced at the wall, distracted by some movement of light there, and noticed that on the wall was a mirror in which he could observe just how thorough a sucking she was performing. Not only that, he could see that there was another mirror above them, behind the headboard of the bed, so that the eager eyes he thought she had been turning on him, actually had been fixed on the mirror. My patient evidently enjoyed watching herself slide the full length of his penis into her clinging lips. He stopped her, not wanting to climax again so quickly, and returned the favor by prodding her sex with his tongue and sucking the juices there. At first he thought she was going to stop him because she pushed her hands furtively down on his head, but he realized that she was just bracing for the ultimate shudder of joy that being kissed there quickly brought to her body.

It went on. And on. She would raise him again when he thought it was impossible to continue, so depleting had the last orgasm been. They tried every position imaginable for at least a stroke or two, enjoying every minute. She even squatted on the dresser, drawing her knees to her chin to expose her vagina to the deepest possible penetration. She danced a waltz across the floor with him inside her. She bicycled her legs in the air while he plunged into her from above.

Finally (Henry said he decided to try it

only because the Julia of the earlier evening had been so disgusted by the thought of it), while she lay there in comfortable exhaustion, face into the incredibly rumpled pillow, a hand still on his penis which she had just eaten completely for the dozenth time, he said, "There's only one other thing," while caressing the well-formed half-spheres of her rump. She didn't respond, but neither did she object when he took the other pillow and slipped it under her stomach to elevate her ass.

There was no particular signal of approval or disapproval. He moved around her and set his groin onto her soft rump, moving to encourage an erection which was by this time slack. He couldn't achieve rigidity enough to penetrate her anus, so after a time he stopped the grinding movement. She reached down with her hand and gripped his penis, tugging in a direction and with firmness that made him follow, crawling on his knees. She pulled him up to her mouth and lazily kissed and sucked at the top of the relaxed organ, which was very pleasant but wasn't having too great an effect at first. So she placed the tip in her mouth and just let it rest there while the juices wetted it to the point of dripping. Then she took it out and just breathed on it, blowing little puffs of breath.

If there is anything that will arouse you to the reality of the life you are sharing in a bed of sex, the breath of a lovely girl on your wet penis will bring about the desired condition. As Henry's penis flexed in response to this treatment, bulging to near fullness almost instantly, Julia nuzzled her lips happily against the tip, keeping them closed but sliding them back and forth. His organ grew as large and firm as ever.

Still she did not let go. She made a slow, attention-getting motion of inserting her index finger into her mouth, wetting it as she had soaked his penis, and, drawing it out, she reached under his testicles and, carefully adjusting her fingernail, slid the finger tantalizingly up his rectum. With an abrupt jerk, his penis seemed to puff out in length and width, and he knew it would never be more ready for action. He moved down to her ass again and she settled there as comfortably as could be. She had given the approval, indeed, the encouragement necessary to go ahead. So, with the feeling of not being able to get enough of this creature, he thrust his organ into the snug but expandable orifice of her rectum.

Julia recoiled momentarily, because a person unaccustomed to anal intercourse *will* have some discomfort in accepting an insertion until they become properly dilated, but after several extremely slow-motion strokes she untensed and seemed to start to enjoy the experience. Anal intercourse usually does not make a woman come, and Henry was so grateful to this splendid woman for the diverse, wild exploitation of their bodies which had taken place that he felt guilty about screwing her in a way which would give him pleasure but would not make her come.

But she seemed to approve, even if not overtly enthusiastic about it, so he continued. However, he made the concession of slipping his hand around the front of her body and settling fingers into her vulva, so that each forward thrust of his penis against her rump brought caresses to her clitoral area too. She very quickly reacted to this, beginning to push back against him as he entered her and to press forward against his hand as he withdrew on the backstroke from her ass. Her own fevered, jerky motions set off such excitement in him that despite what should have been a completely drained condition, he found himself approaching the full, breathless, gasping climax in the briefest of intervals. When he finally let go inside her, it was so complete that—like an overworked peasant fearful of being ordered to do more labor—his penis immediately shrank itself right out of her, as though saying, "That's it; that's all that I can do tonight; it's closing time."

Julia didn't talk much as they dressed, but the skin of her body virtually radiated the female quality; she glowed. Even though disheveled by ardor, with her hair mussed, her makeup streaked, her lipstick wiped clear off, her face glistening with moisture, her expression tainted by physical weariness, and even her posture suffering from the wobbly condition of depletion, she was more beautiful than she had been at any time that evening.

Back in the living room again, Julia reclined on the couch, while Henry got a cocktail to refresh her. People began looking at them as if to say, "Where in hell did you two disappear all night?" It was two o'clock in the morning. He had said hello to her shortly after eight. The thing that struck him most about the whole transformance of this vibrant, lovely woman was that when he returned with the drink, another man was standing there talking to her and she was coldly replying, with tight-lipped displeasure, "I don't believe in free sex, no, not at all. To me, you *have* to be *in love* with a person, or it's just meaningless sex."

Hearing these words and seeing her frown in pristine disdain at the interloper, my acquaintance sighed a great sigh of appreciation for Julia, who sat there looking exactly as she had a half dozen hours before, although now with the aroma of sex still clinging to her wonderful body. If a preacher had come along at that moment and shouted, "Hail to the glory of love," Henry would have answered, "Yea, brethren, amen."

As a psychologist, the most significant facet to me of this sexual adventure, which is forever imprinted on my friend's mind because he can never stop extolling the virtues of Julia as the best damn lay he ever had in his life, is that Julia was coming to me for therapy to solve a curious problem that was ruining her marriage: she was frigid. At least, with her husband she was frigid, a situation which is not too rare, kind of a highly selective frigidity. Aside from that clinical sidelight, the interesting thing was the "love" made possible such a Mrs. Jeckle-Miss Hyde alteration of the girl.

Of course, any man who experiences a girl in such a memorable incident really does love her, and she him. Their story is almost a classic illustration of the point that no man can ever accept at face value a word a woman says until he knows precisely on what terms she means what she says, and that "love" is a password in America. Girls who are supposedly paragons of purity and virtue, abiding by every strict admonition of their parents, teachers, and church, practicing total abstinence from physical sex despite almost overpowering urges to the contrary, will throw all caution to the wind, brush aside lifelong training and the direct fears of punishment from an irate Supreme Being, parent, or society—all in the name of love. Despite everything they have been taught, they can suddenly shed their clothes and hurl their bodies into feasts of passion, and if anybody reminds them of the change in their behavior, it can be shrugged off with, "But I love him—"

Thankfully, the same society that created such passive repressions, tearing people emotionally apart and stunting the sex life of most of its citizens, left one ticket to the gates of freedom and called it love. Well, who wouldn't love Julia? And there are thousands of Julias. So many that the human spirit must be looked upon with admiration and love when one sees that despite years of rigid indoctrination and threats of retaliation against all those who deviate from the dictates of puritanical society, men and women survive. Not only do they survive, but they find freedom on their own. And once they have experienced it and know what it means, they will not be denied it any further.

Those who learn to love, to really appreciate the femininity and personal qualities of the women they lay, and it is not difficult for any thinking man (no matter how thoroughly some women camouflage their beauty, it is there) to learn to appreciate these qualities, these men have already taken a major step toward realizing their ultimate sensual powers, for the mind is perhaps the greatest of sex tools.

Although the word love, and the act of saying, "I love you," figure strongly in our prime example above, it is the emotion of love we are dealing with and not an unreal mask of it, for the magic words uttered by Julia to make the frigid girl disappear represent a deep emotion on her part. To the sensuous mind, the ideal situation is to lay every girl you love, and love every girl you lay.

CHAPTER VIII

YOUR OTHER TOOLS OF SEX

Now that we have counted two basic tools of male sex expression, the penis and the mind, and the glorious interrelation of imagination and memory on that vibrant, fleshy instrument, there are several other faculties of the human organism which should be brought into play in delivering physical love to another human. Your sense of touch: Your tongue. Enjoying your sense of smell. The joy of hearing sex spoken. Deriving happiness as a voyeur.

Touch is perhaps the most important, because that is what love-making is all about; it is physical contact. Of course you can touch with your lips, your penis, your tongue, and even your feet, but the prime implements for touch, as intended by the design of the human organism, are your hands. For something different in a touch treat, by the way, try sometime at a rather idle moment in your love play the practice of gently fondling your woman's breasts with your feet and toes, and slide your toes sideways into the lips of her vulva—but be sure your nails are trimmed. Did you ever consider how many men have gone through their entire lives without ever once experiencing the pleasurable embrace of a woman hugging her breasts against your rump in mutual massage, or your testicles, or, for that matter, the tender tissue at the back of your knees?

The use of touch in expressing love is practically limitless. Think about it a moment. You are in a fabulously expensive treasure storehouse in distant Hong Kong, and the most dear (which originally meant costly, by the way) object of all has been pressed into your hands for your admiration. It is an elaborately carved jade goddess, so smooth to the touch that it feels fluid. You must run your hands over it to appreciate it. You touch and trace the intricate tresses etched into the hair; you poke into the provocative small of her back; you rest a fingerprint against the facial features to feel the fine details of the face; you awe at the translucent, thin extremeties. The respect you pay this article which has no life is pure admiration, and that is what you give a woman when you touch her. To hold her, caress her, stroke her, manipulate her flesh, squeeze her breasts, run fingers through her hair, all these touches are the same form of admiration.

Your hands are telling her she is beautiful and desirable, which women love to be told. Warmed by your appraisal of them, they will pay you with the effort to be as beautiful physically as you wish them to be, which can bring all manner of delights.

One of the most unfortunate omissions in love-making is the loss of appreciation for human touching, a tactic that the sensual male must develop to its fullest possibilities. Morality inherited and handed down to us still tends to cling to the hands off, don't maul me attitude, and many a woman can be heard to say it, "I don't like to be mauled; don't paw me."

Too bad. One of my recent patients was a teenager who had a very severe problem of adjusting to life, a problem which she had tried to solve by promiscuous activity before coming to me. "Sam" was her name, but despite the appellation she was an extremely feminine person, in looks and feeling. She was the kind of girl about whom callous men would comment, "She'll screw anything with pants on." Of course she would. She was desperate for love and approval and she wasn't getting it. But at least those who would not hug and hold her with their arms *would* press their bodies on and into her, and it was token enough at the time.

I haven't mentioned Sam's basic problem, but for a reason. She was an average teenager, unafraid of emotion instinctively but raised with the usual restrictions of the culture. She told me that when she was in school she had a boyfriend and while "necking" with him one night in his car (which was permitted by teenage code even for good girls and Sam was a virgin then) she wanted him to feel her breasts, because, being prohibited, she was intrigued at just what was this forbidden sensation. But her boyfriend knew she wasn't "that kind of girl," and wouldn't do anything like that to her, even though he, too, would have liked to. She didn't vocalize her wish, of course, because nice girls didn't do that, but she had decided that if he got up the nerve to try, then she would let him, with, of course, the proper number of unconvincing protests.

Damn, it, though, he didn't try. The closest he got was to place his hand on her shoulder, at the collarbone, and there it stayed. She eyed the angle and then turned her body so that the hand dropped, and with her calculation of the trajectory being correct, the hand fell on her breast. So he looked into her eyes and found them blank but couldn't pull away. She got the molesting that she desired, her boyfriend even getting brave enough to dart inside her dress to the flesh, and she loved every minute of it. He paid the price, however, refusing to see her for weeks, guilty at having taken advantage of her and fearful that he, monster that he was, was despoiling the virginal creature with his lust. The point is, she was a girl who appreciated the sensation of being touched, which contributed a great deal to her problem.

The last time she was making love with a man, she told me, he stroked her crotch, inserted his finger there, and, of course, touched her breasts and nipples, stroked the crease in her back and even pleasurably mauled her fleshy rump. Her experience does make a comment on the sad state of tactile exploration, however, as she said with mixed emotion: "It wasn't until I got right over his face for sixty-nine, with my pussy in his mouth, that he realized I had a wooden leg!"

She had lost the leg in an accident, and, being young and beautiful, sought to affirm in repeated love affairs that she was still desirable despite her artificial limb. She regained her confidence when she realized that even in the intimacy of the bedroom, men often failed to realize they were making love to a one-legged girl!

Such a condition comes about through years of practicing insensitivity. One man told me—it was not necessarily related to his role as a patient other than that he was boasting of his ability to turn on a chick ridden by inhibitions—how he was saying goodnight to a girl in his car, in the darkness of her driveway, and, after an hour, she became very passionate. She was a virgin of course—this was years ago before the species happily declined to the state of rarity.

She wore protective slacks, the better to guard what was referred to as a girl's MPP, most prized possession, if you understand the frame of reference. Despite her adamant moral objection to expressing sexuality, she found herself panting and hot, and so pent up that she had to let go. They were practically horizontal in the front seat. She took the initiative in clinging to his neck, while he plucked at the disarray of her blouse to fondle her breasts.

She shifted her crotch into contact with his knee. Pressing there, pushing her hot little sex against that knee, gave her such a thrill of relief that she began long, greedily pleasurable thrusts of her loins against his knee, reaching a point so close to hurling her life-long codes to the wind that she was actually swinging it there, thumping at it, trying to come.

At this point, he, being a gentleman as well as a child of the times, decided to assist her in her modest sex spree, reaching a hand down to cup the back of her firmly rounded ass. It was the least he could do. She sighed a heavy sigh, savoring it as she came. Lifting her crotch from his knee, which somehow had gotten a wet spot on it, she gave him a searchingly cold stare of compelling disgust. With all the flourish of a hero expelling the villain or the virgin bravely baring her breast to accept death before dishonor, she reached down to that offending hand he had with such brazen lust placed on her sacred left bun and extricated it with all the repugnance of an exterminator evicting a rat by the tail.

I had to wonder if she was ever able to become a good lay in later years, because she did have a certain native drive which might have conquered her deadly upbringing under the proper conditions. I never asked, but I assumed that he, the bangee with the dry-humped knee, masturbated that night, if he hadn't already come in his fly with sheer joy at the magnanimousness of this lovely, warm girl consenting to become so intimate with him as to get her gun in his presence, thereby admitting the possibility of womanhood in front of his very eyes.

The sensuous male must practice touch, the sensation of feeling, to rekindle the lost art. Touch cloth, touch steel, touch grass, touch leaves, the bark of trees, the grain of cut wood, paper, plastic, fur, glass, leather, raw meat. Touch coarse things and cold things, multi-dimensional things. Touch sound, the vibrations of music against an amplifier's mouth. Touch velvet and burlap and wool. Look at things, pick them up and touch them. Practice. Learn to differentiate textures by touch, with your eyes closed.

And when you have learned to marvel at how things feel, then you can practice your tactile accomplishments on the flesh of a human female. You can run your hands, the palm and the fingers, down the small of her back and touch the Venus dimples there. Touch every surface and crevice and opening of her as though you were a blind man on a strange planet trying to determine the proportions of a creature you had encountered after a long, solitary journey. If you practice this continually you will acquire the faculty of expressing love with your hands as overtly as the miser who sifts his hands through his beloved money.

There are peripheral benefits to touching a woman. If you rub her back you relax her muscles and help prepare her to release herself from within that enclosure of skin. When your hand stirs the flesh it heightens circulation in the thousand channels of real blood coursing through that body and brings to her a flush of desire. As you caress the spine your fingertips limber up the nerves running from her brain to her crotch, signalling that they should prepare for the flood of feeling from stimulated nerve endings, and that begins when at last you sink your tremulous grip into the damp and redolent wellspring of her sexual activity. You touch her body and memorize it. When your brain stores up the knowledge of every inch of her humanity and womanhood, it is amazing how your own mind can set your body aflame and spur you on to greater passion.

One last word about the benefits which accrue to he who touches, because the incident serves to bridge our way to another tool of sex. Recently, a man who comes to me for therapy told me of a social encounter with a woman who had the most exemplary pair of breasts that he had ever seen, even considering the widespread exposure of females in the advertisements, film, television and magazines in this breast-oriented culture of ours. Never had he seen such perfection. Her figure was generally good, and her face interesting. She dressed well, playing up her mammary excellence to the hilt. To see them was to long to touch them and suck them.

Through some chance of fate, he found himself in a bedroom with this possessor of the ultimate breasts one night, and ripped his clothes off with haste so as to observe and savor that tragically human moment when she unlatched those daringly molded curves from their halter and, expectedly, let them drop. They were big enough to lead a life of their own so, naturally, the instant the bra was let loose the breasts would sag, wouldn't they? His eyes were pinned there in amazement as she discarded her upper lingerie and those two darling glands barely jostled, standing as firm and independent and jutting as the buns of her very solid ass.

He couldn't get over it. She assumed the horizontal position and, as she lay back, again instead of flattening of their own weight and dispersing to some extent, they protruded upward with such self-assertion that he swore they were reaching for him. The ultimate breasts.

His hands, both of them, moved to seize these creatures without further delay, but again he was taken aback, and, alas, disappointingly so. They were as hard and unyielding as baseballs. Even lying atop them they did not give, so that he was balanced somewhat precariously there, a very unusual sensation.

The explanation was that she had been a Las Vegas showgirl of the breast-baring variety and later received some local acclaim as a topless dancer, a career during which she felt it necessary to insure her assets by having a silicone job. It's not really visible; plastic surgeons insert in the breasts silicone discs, cone-shaped, in a now obsolete operation. Those plastic breasts will still be standing up straight when she barely can. The point of this little anecdote is that, for touch, there is nothing like female flesh, but visual inspiration is a whole separate bag.

The visual element of any sexual encounter is as vital as touch, if not more so, for the brain stores its sexual experiences as though they were color film, with the images able to be summoned upon command by the memory, a key supplier of the ingredients which build vibratingly hard erections in preparation for new memories.

From the start your eyes examine fully clothed the creature whom you hope to lay.

Although in the first blush of intimacy she may not dare the complication of a fully exposed sex experience, light being possibly an inhibiting factor at that juncture, there must come a point when to all the other sensations of the sexual experience the visual influence is added. To enjoy sex with all the lights blazing, peeking down to view your organ disappearing into her, savoring the beauty of her face and figure and the expressions that passion bring, these are delights not to be neglected.

Once the lights have been turned on, you will be moving in an interesting direction if you try sex with mirrors, large expanses of mirror that give both you and your partner full-length views of yourselves in the process of copulating and other assorted sexual practices, the variations sometimes being inspired by the fact that for the first time a person can see what they themselves look like naked in bed involved in the ultimate expression of their sexuality.

A friend of mine had a large, private bedroom suite in his Hollywood Hills home and it had such an alignment of mirrors that the bedroom, which he generally made available to people interested in trying out the visual sensation, became a virtual circus of activity; every twosome privately engaged in their devotions became a virtual orgy of images, as though the whole world were copying them. Unfortunately, as couples gradually learned, the reason this friend was so generous in sharing his bedroom of glass and its multiplicity of sensual images was that he also had the mirrors rigged to provide for observation. Persons could excuse themselves to go to the bathroom upstairs and, without disturbing the couple engaged in sexual activity, watch their every action reflected in the hall.

This voyeurism, at which he was rarely caught because of the handy excuse of just passing by on his way to the bathroom, sometimes reached the point where a couple who thought they were alone and were disporting themselves in shameless sexual athletics for the sake of the mirrors, actually were being watched by a half dozen other people, fully dressed, standing in the unlit hallway. Of course, voyeurism and exhibitionism can go hand in hand by fortunate coincidence. One couple, the story goes, even though they had discovered that their naked sexual activity was being watched by others, returned to the bedroom on another night to put on a more inspired show than the first time.

Visible sex does have its outer limits, but as a general rule, the more a couple can see of each other while engaged in each other, the better. A colleague told me of a case which, although by no means rare, did display a destructive inclination. He was a marriage counselor and one couple who came to him during the last shaky moments of a shattering marriage had pursued visual sex to the extremes. They were both beautiful people, very talented, perfect physical specimens and, outwardly at least, very self-confident and outgoing. Inwardly, they were both terrifyingly unsure of their own sexual identity. Now, while he chose one way to deny the unsureness and grope for identity, she chose another, but they managed to do it together.

Their bedroom was walled on two sides with mirrors and was lighted as brightly as an all night coffee shop on the highway. The woman, a curvaceous thing at what should have been the peak of her sexual life, liked to assert superfemininity by taking on two men at a time, and since the man liked to demonstrate his prowess by coming twice in a row, they worked out a fairly regular experience in which she would lay on her back or stomach, head to the side, orally stimulating her husband while a male friend penetrated her.

The excitement of watching his own wife being laid (and, since he was simultaneously experiencing the oral sensation, it was like detaching from reality and observing himself penetrating her, an image reduplicated in mirrors) made it easy for him to come in her mouth and arise again to attend the other end of her, copying what he had just seen. And since she was actually unsure of her femininity, she needed the second pubic arousal to bring her to full orgasmic completion.

This couple's practice was not done on recommendation of their psychologist, and might not be the best approach for anyone with an unstable sexual identity or any other kind of marital difficulties, it should be pointed out.

One visual stimulus which is heartily recommended for all is that which can be undertaken with the very handy and inexpensive Polaroid camera. Using either a timer or a cable extension for the shutter, couples can pose themselves in a variety of close-up or full-length sexual pictures, using flash in the privacy of their own bedroom and creating their own pornography. There is no film to be sent out for the edifying chuckles of the developer-technician and camera store clerks and their friends, so it all stays at home; you do have to remember that the film creates a negative which is usable, so the negatives must be destroyed unless you don't mind chancing the publicity.

One charming but devastatingly hung-up woman whom I treated for a time complained one day about her husband's preoccupation with such pornography. She did not mind posing with him, doing anything and everything, even sequence shots showing the penis at various stages of entry into her vagina or mouth. In fact she snapped most of them by extension cable, he being preoccupied with positioning his penis—which she had to administer to until it was at its prime, preened like an actor getting ready to go on.

But what she did object to was his hangup with fate games—the idea of a controlling force outside of themselves, which made sex a bit more thrilling if it was carried out as though ordered, like a command from someone else forcing them to do it. When they had acquired over the months of orgasms an extensive collection of poses of themselves, he would initiate their regular sex activity by drawing out the stack of pictures like a deck of cards, face down, and she would pick one. Whatever was on the picture, they would do.

Well, she found the system interesting enough to experiment with one time, but he wanted to do it that way all the time. She felt it too restricting. She wanted to suck him when she felt the urge, not when the pictures—take a card, any card—said so. And besides, since he had posed a preponderance of oral sex experiences, it was ending up that he was getting oral orgasms a lot more regularly than she was getting vaginal thrills, which was what she wanted most.

We all have our problems. Although oral sex activity will be examined with considerably more detail in a later chapter, the tongue as a tool of sex certainly cannot fail to receive honorable mention. The tongue is particularly important in love-making and it should be cultivated so that you are able to use it as much as possible during sexual acts.

Kissing is one of the best turn-ons that man has devised. With the exception of the hair, where it might get sticky, there is hardly a place on the female body where the hands can go that the tongue cannot follow. Some women actually prefer sixty-nine to regular copulation because the touch of the slightly coarse, moist tongue on their clitoris drives them wild. This sport has become so popular that one imaginative company is now marketing fruit-flavored douches for women to give it an appealing strawberry, raspberry or lime taste.

If you have not yet learned to move your tongue with ease, it is advisable that you start practicing, and a good way to develop its powers is to stick it out as far as you can, retracting it and sticking it out repeatedly for ten times a day. In a very brief time you will find that you can stick your tongue out much farther than you could initially.

The next time you kiss a girl rotate your tongue around her tongue inside her mouth a few times. Suck her tongue into your mouth and twirl your tongue around hers again. As indicated, this class in tongue-lashing love will meet again at the female crotch in a later chapter, but for now suffice it to say that just as you can learn to feel your woman, you can learn to taste her, all over her body.

In case you want to entice her to do the same, by the way, even though I am not aware of a candy-flavored penis coating on the market, there are people who have tried chocolate syrup, ice cream, wine, whipped cream and a dozen other tempting taste delights which can be applied liberally to the penis and licked off by eager lips. But watch out for girls who are counting their calories, who by the way can be advised of the latest American Medical Association report that the caloric content of male semen is virtually non-existent. Chemically, it is almost pure protein, which makes it ideal food, certainly not harmful to swallow and actually nourishing and good. Unless your sex partner is a gourmet, or needs some special masquerade to attract her lips to your penis, it is perhaps best to stick with a good masculine scent of the slightly spicy variety, not too sweet, a lotion rather than a perfume.

The idea of perfume brings up another manner of appreciating your woman's body and your sex relations with her—that is, your nose, which can savor every part of her undiluted by artificial scents. One girl I know is always in very high demand—or her crotch is, actually. Because she has arrived at the most delicious combination of spicy odor blended with the aroma of her sex, men are waiting in line for a chance to bury their noses in her vulva, a sexual practice which pleases her most, fittingly enough.

The only thing I can't understand is how a girl who comes as much as she does could have arrived at any regulated proportion for mixing the Eau de Chanel with the eau de sex. One of the mysteries of life worth exploring, with your nose. Of course, some people fire up their olfactory senses by burning incense or aromatic candles. On the other hand, unless you are carrying on an affair in an outhouse, the natural odor of your bodies and sex is more preferable and stimulating than most anything that could be sprayed in the air.

The foregoing paragraph naturally is aimed at regular bathers and grants full dispensation to any male with an orgiastic hangup over some special perfume on the female body, which is, after all, very female.

Chances are that if you can get all those senses going simultaneously—touching, tasting, viewing and appraising with your nostrils, plus bringing in the previously mentioned aspects of memory and loving appreciation—you will come off without further attention from your female before your penis even touches her. But all of these faculties were provided to you for your enjoyment of life and they will certainly elevate the pleasure of sex to new heights. As for the danger of experiencing orgasm by virtue of the external stimuli alone, that is the very reason why you have been provided in a previous chapter with numerous methods of delaying the climax.

Lastly, there is the auditory contribution

to the enjoyment of sex, and here the reference is not to any specific selection of conducive music which might be called "The Copulation Concerto." In practice, music is a good build-up, but can turn out to be a distraction when you are trying to apply all your senses to the body you are sharing love with. For those who have never experienced the joy of hearing sex spoken, what we mean are words. Sexually liberated and secure males and females often find verbal, graphic descriptions and words of encouragement quite stimulating. It will vary from woman to woman and, lacking experience in any isolated instance, it is perhaps prudent to let the female's utterances be your guide.

The point is, any woman will purr in response to repeated whispers, "You're beautiful, God, you're beautiful," which are the cautious orisons of a man kneeling in worship at the altar. If words do arouse her, then proceed with the devotionals and pay verbal tribute to the warmth of her body, praise the brilliant vision of her skin flashing under you, utter specific progress reports on the effect her unparalleled steamy sexuality is having on your body and its production of semen. Or, if all you *can* do is recite "The Raven," for God's sake keep quiet. Which is not to be taken as a commandment of sex, for there are circumstances under which it might even be wise to recite "The Raven."

The point is that you should never be

afraid to laugh in bed or admit in clearer syllables that what you are doing is engaging in fun. Laughter is relaxing and sometimes there is an indication that tension is too great. Maybe your partner is too uptight and a laugh will let her enjoy herself, or start to. On the other hand, if she is liberated and you are too, she may choose earthier, less poetic expressions which will endear her nonetheless. At the height of activity if she begins moaning, "Oh, fuck me, fuck me, fuck me, come, come, come–" then you can be sure she has no need to interpret her current activity as a spiritual experience.

You can trade with her the jargon of the liberated bed–"pussy, prick, cunt, stick it way in, suck me"–all are terms which have a currency in bed. If you are ever going to stick your prick into a pussy, it is going to be in bed, not in some book, and in the heat of passion, if you should be formal enough to declare, "I'll insert my penile member into your vagina now," she may send you to the blackboard to draw a diagram.

CHAPTER IX

UNDISCOVERED SEXUAL GOLD MINES

Whenever a patient tells me that he or she is having trouble meeting members of the opposite sex, I know immediately that there is something wrong with their entire pattern of living, or their approach to living. After all, the world is roughly half and half males and females, depending on your age group, and for younger males, the ratio is getting better all the time. Since this situation exists, then if you do not happen to be in some peculiar position such as serving with the submarine forces in the polar region, you should be encountering your fair share of females in the normal pursuit of your daily life.

And if you really are conducting a search for compatible members of the opposite sex, then you obviously should be meeting *more* than your fair share. What happens in too many cases is that the person really is not looking, is over-looking, or is looking in the wrong places. This chapter, while not conceding any such thing as the possibility that there are not enough women who desire the ultimate communication with the sensuous male, does try to illustrate at least a dozen different approaches to finding situations in which you are surrounded by women seeking the same thing you are.

In any normal situation in society, the self-possessed man who is a competent sensualist will, in the course of his work, his transportation, or his recreation, be exposed to many women. He shouldn't have to try too hard, because, unless told otherwise by gestures of rejection or being completely ignored, women are always alert for sex signals. We are talking about those delectable creatures who engineer their most visible female insignia, their breasts, into halters that not only aim right at you, but approach you before any other part of them does.

These are the repositories of love who walk with their elbows back and their hands fluttering at hip level like fine embroidery edging a delicate silk. From the age of thirteen they devote a major portion of their time, money and thoughts to matters which in repose are all reduced to their pelvic region. That applies whether it is a new eyebrow pencil, a job they take for sexual exposure, or a man they size up as a possible husband.

Some people will argue that women don't pursue sex, they pursue security, permanence. No, they pursue *sex* with security, *sex* with permanence. And you have to be mightily consumed by the pursuit of sex to seek it within a secure, permanent arrangement, so that you'll always have it.

In the past few years I have received in my office an increasing stream of young married women who, having abided by the teachings and traditions of a bygone era, went to their marriage beds as virgins. Today, no matter how good their sex life is at home, their marriages are suffering an extreme stress because either they or their husbands—and it usually is the woman—are saying, as one finely dressed young matron declared, irritatedly setting fire to a cigarette, "I could kick myself in the ass every time I think of all the chances I had and let them go."

The jargon of the psychologist refers to this phenomenon as "pussy fever." At least we in the profession refer to it informally in those terms when we get together and compare notes and try (for the sake of our own sanity) to chuckle at the folly of human nature. Oh my patron saints of fertility, I have to shake my head in compassion (while trying to smile nonetheless) at the greatness of the human spirit in trying to break out of the sexual cage it has created in the name of nicety.

For generations middle-class girls considered it a point of honor to return home from a date with their undergarments intact. For every pair of panties unremoved, there was a fly unzipped and two minds left in turmoil. While their bodies and instincts and desires told them yes, yes, now, now, they could not, would not, and did not. When I think of all that love undone, I know why my office is filled with wonderful people, their warmth buried yet, who cannot understand the bald-faced lie they have been living.

The lie forced them to deny their feelings for all their formative years until, with the mumbling of what they were told were sacrosanct words by preacher, prelate or civic official, they supposedly were set free to open the floodgates of passion. Then they wonder where all their passion went, they wonder why they resent their mutual captivity. Feelings, sensuality, and love must be practiced openly and constantly to develop.

How could they develop when the barricades of passion are thrown up at the breast level—"Just touch them, all right?"—and love is restrained to a mind which fully weighs all practical considerations and other inculcated, learned measures of approval? Usually this lesson in repression occurred during their teen years, when feelings are just emerging, just begging to be learned, and are of savage intensity.

So, men, there is a whole generation of

women out there, repenting at their wastefulness, their miserliness in failing to squander their milk-ripe passions. Now, panicky at the fear of advancing age, and liberated by the pill, they long for a chance to make up for it. They are practically standing atop buildings like mad millionaires guilty of hoarding, screaming and throwing fistsfull of money to the crowds. It is the considered sociological duty of the sensitive American male to give refuge in the nearest bed to every one of those disconsolate creatures who has escaped from bondage and comes crawling for help like a fugitive from her morals. She is not guilty. Love her. Love her till her sex organs ache with joy.

Which brings us to the first fertile ground of lusting women, found in that simple truth roaring at us from the ages of antiquity: Love thy neighbor.

This is not a suggestion to go from door to door through the suburbs selling sexual freedom. You may get laid, but more likely you'll get arrested, or mechanically punctured by some armed husband who has not caught the spirit of the age. The point is that you should go to the suburbs by daylight, when women are most alone and lonely. You go to the stores, the businesses, restaurants, and diurnal recreation centers of the suburbs. You participate in the games of the suburbs, civic causes, group activities, political movements, petition drives, card playing, Good Samaritanship and general helpfulness, not only because it makes a better, nobler man of you, but because it all ends up in bed. If you get involved with situations in the suburbs, you will become involved with the people, including the females who need so much sympathetic attention.

Just because we are talking about sex as fun, which in all candor is the thing that most people like about it, doesn't mean we are taking a callous point of view such as the unfeeling generation past, which handed down the frustrations and lies described above, and who regarded women as "pieces of ass." If you rock the body of a woman for an hour, and love her humanity for that hour, even if you never see each other again, you have not only cleaned out your pipes, drained your sweat glands, expended calories and anxieties and brought a smile to your face and hers, but you have shared love, and it's something to remember. There is nothing more moral.

The sensuous male learns to feel, and the feeling man sympathizes with and loves his neighbor. Oh yes, I know full well that there will be women who talk too much or have other disturbing habits. What man hasn't had an experience like this: You meet a voluptuous woman, perhaps at a party. She has long black hair falling down the middle of her back and the finely chiseled features of a Grecian statue, with a complexion of white marble. Breathlessly, eagerly you press for that long delayed moment when you maneuver her into the bedroom and she strips.

While lying there naked, displaying an almost flawless white physique that lights up the dark room with its cool glow, she persists in moaning of her daily life's problems, an ailment or two, or even revealing that she is pregnant, or has dandruff. It may even reach the point where, your sensuous powers throbbing, you could scream, "For Chrissakes, shut up!" Instead, by not responding verbally, but with caresses, you get her to quietly cling to you, which is what she wants, and in your resulting fiery sexual union she will display all the groping, clutching fervor of her need for another human to feel what she felt.

I have described a beautiful woman; naturally it detracts from the masculine fantasy of perfect beauty to have the splendid creature expose a mind fraught with commonplace human problems, and do it on the very brink of sexual intercourse. But to the extent that it makes her more human, your ardor can be heightened. After all, this is not a two-dimensional cinema image, nor a cold statue you are piercing with your swollen penis: it is a creature of flesh and blood and emotion and desire. You can feel it by becoming aware of it. Your caresses should try to tell her you know this.

Every man deserves the right and the

privilege at least once in his life of enjoying to utter delight a fantastically beautiful woman. But the truly sensual male does not require model-type perfection to appease his desire. In reality there may be more human warmth, willingness, lust and versatility in a fat girl, but it's harder to get out. Never set standards of human perfection that hinge on external physical appearance alone, or you will rob yourself of half of life, and rob them, too.

Some historians maintain that Cleopatra, the arch-temptress of all time, was not a particularly good-looking girl. Her beauty came out in the bedroom where her total humanness exploded in passion and feeling so delicate and experienced that any man who ever touched her could never forget what she did to him. These are the invisible treasures that are everywhere around you.

Does she have imperfections? Her hair isn't right, perhaps? Her breasts too pendulous? All breasts are victims of gravity sooner or later, which is why so many vibrant girls of centerfold magazine exposure are always posing magnificently with their arms reaching up in the air; it is not to grasp sky but to elevate flesh. Is her ass a bit too large? Her voice a bit too coarse? If you pass by every creature who fails to meet a set of market-value specifications, you are cheating yourself, for the less-than-perfect humans are the majority of the human race, and are the ones who are striving hardest for perfection.

Too many ideal beauties, narcissistic in their self-adoration, are unable to demonstrate love for others because they don't really feel it. Besides, they don't want to ruffle the perfection of their selves with the exertions required by lovemaking. Don't deprive yourself by failing to see beauty in every female; it is there. Searching for beauty in the less than perfect opens a whole new field of sexual exploration.

By the nature of human growth it must be recognized that the most overweight of women was at some magic instant in her life, for some fleeting instant, perhaps, the possessor of a perfect body. Behind every plain face there is a hunger to be beautiful, and the man who can make that woman believe she is beautiful is going to be rewarded with the most enduring display of sexual gratitude that woman has ever given to man.

Returning, however, to fertile hunting grounds, I will enumerate ten, merely as examples. They are really too numerous, as numerous in fact as all the miles of earth that women walk, their pubic mounds thrust out in provocative slacks or their bikini-clad private orifice bared below to the creatures of the grass under their skirts.

For both the confident and the timid and the searcher after self, there are nudist colonies where the body is taken so much for granted that when feelings occur between two people, expression of the feelings physically also is taken for granted. This is not to say that most nudist colonies are havens for the sexually ever-active. Not at all. Some, being among the earliest of liberal groups, do advocate that not only is there nothing to be hidden about the human body, but the same applies to *all* its functions.

By the way, as for the nakedness, whatever your own body looks like, you will find in nudist camps that most bodies are rather average specimens of flesh, and that unflawed characteristics are rare. But these people are not afraid to display their humanity. Investigate. Many have visitor plans and resort vacation-type programs. If, perchance, you fear that the sight of all that nakedness will cause you to be constantly erect and therefore embarrassed, forget it. Unless physically stimulated, the chances of your getting an erection at all are psychologically infinitesimal.

Encounter groups are a big thing the last few years, groups which are planned to help you experience deeper feelings, groups which explore the sensitivity of touch, or try to draw out each person's inner resentments and problems which tend to restrict human sensitivity. Look into these groups, but check them quite thoroughly, talking to people who have experienced sessions with them. To say the least, some are better than others, depending on their leader, his qualifications and the group's goal. If you like what they are trying to do, the way they go about it, and the kind of people who participate, try it. You will not only be perhaps sharpening your sensitivity, but you will be mixing with an open-minded group of people of a type you would like.

Religions are a hotbed of sexual delight, for a very specific psychological reason. The women in them, and especially in the more enlightened religions which stress free human thought rather than second-hand commands from God, tend to feel more comfortable with men who are churchgoers like they are. They have the same physical urges and equipment as all females, and they feel more receptive, less threatened by men they meet on church grounds than they would be with others, feeling a bond already has been established. There has been an enormous amount of inspired sexual passion initiated with the implied blessing of an unvocal deity, and most assuredly he would approve if asked. These are his creatures, which he constructed for this ritual of love, and in philosophical law, there is no good without action; the absence of action is the absence of good.

For city dwellers I'm going to make an exception to my general abhorrence of clubs, which tend to dissipate more energy than they create, and suggest a possible fertile ground or two. Organizations like Parents Without Partners, and there are several, national in scope, consist of a membership of mostly women who have lost their husbands, plus an unbalanced percentage of males. One fellow I knew flashed his nephew's picture for admission. The education didn't hurt him and he met a female he later married. Be careful not to take unfair advantage, with so many women used to regular sex lives and now deprived, and, although most of them are looking for new husbands, they are a sensible lot and are more reluctant to commit another rash marital mistake than to satisfy what they have come to recognize as a healthy urge.

For basically similar reasons, the Women's Liberation movement is actually an excellent hunting ground for sex partners. Of course, males can't join most groups, which are dedicated to overpowering men as leaders of the world, a feat which was accomplished in 200 A.D. But the members are people with inquisitive minds, questioning outdated principals and, even though their detractors accuse the Womlibs of being less than feminine, it is a psychologically known fact that beautiful women who do have homosexual tendencies often overcompensate by performing like wildcats in bed. It is a service of man to the cause that he permit these women to demonstrate that they certainly are not frigid, no matter what people think.

One of the prime territories for approaching the sexually minded female in an altogether altruistic manner is to frequent gyms, health clubs and health-oriented resorts which are organized on the presumption that some sort of physical betterment will result from attending. You see, not only will you probably do yourself the favor of achieving some measure of physical improvement, but you will be mixing with women who are seeking to improve themselves physically. If they have come to recognize the desirability of this, and are doing it, their reason is rooted in discontent with their current power to attract. The male who is on hand to be first to let them demonstrate their new allure is due for a massage he'll never forget.

From professional involvements, it has been my observation through the years that there is an extraordinary number of attractive women frequenting courthouses in America. While my research has not been thorough enough at this point to flatly declare that great beauty attracts trouble with the law, I have isolated the fact that it is mostly their men who are being accused, tried and sentenced, leaving behind a beauteous creature in need of sympathy and consolation, pledging undying faithfulness, no doubt. But for the adventuresome it is only a matter of time and understanding.

The difficulty in drawing conclusions regarding the creatures who frequent these halls of justice is compounded by the fact that so many attractive secretarial workers have determinedly enveigled their personnages into the office staffs, which they consider an ideal hunting spot for capturing professional men: lawyers, that is, not burglars. The cafeterias where secretaries go to lunch are not bad hunting grounds, by the way; many secretaries today are surprisingly liberated of course by the pill. If you have a credit card and take them to lunch in a first-rate restaurant, you have brushed aside any economic barriers that may have existed to prevent your going to bed together.

Reading is one interesting form of female hunting and the want ads can be a source of considerable intrigue and imaginative pursuit. One friend of mine, who does not own a business but has lots of spare time, constantly runs a professional-type ad for young women to work part time in his office. Since part-time work is probably most in demand, he has a constant stream of women visiting him for interviews. Since the jobs do not exist, this may be less than honest, but on the other hand he is giving them some experience in being interviewed, and giving them a chance to meet interesting people—him. Some are bought lunch, dinner, and, of course, breakfast. And if they really are desperate for work, he tries to keep track of openings elsewhere for them.

If you have a trade or profession that you could spread to the suburbs on a part-time basis or per job, a cleverly worded ad can send you on interesting calls. Be careful, though, to stick to the letter of the law and the implied contract between employer and employee. It's just a way of meeting people. Or, conversely, if someone else is advertising, you can go job hunting, whether you want one or not.

Finally, also getting your lead from newspaper reading, you can find the greatest assemblage of beauty-conscious women in any town by following the big sales—"Fantastic bargains—50% Off"—at fashionable clothing stores. Never go in with the first wave, when the ladies are known to be in a hypnotic trance and wouldn't recognize a nude male in a fitting room. After the first two hours, when a cup of coffee would be a welcome offer to the shoppers, is the best time. Ladies clothing departments, and don't forget lingerie, are the busiest, most fertile arenas, and even if you never get a word of encouragement from anyone, just mixing with the perfumed bodies—"Excuse me," as you smile and sidle past between a round rump and a soft thigh—should provide entertainment.

We have listed about a dozen specific occasions and locations for the nearness of women, and the list could go on and on. But the sensuous male, if he attunes his sexual antenna toward beauty, will find it everywhere. It is there, everywhere. The trick is to recognize and appreciate it.

CHAPTER X

SEXUAL ECONOMICS

One facet of sexual reality that seldom is examined is the matter of economics. The world we live in has forced us all to become creatures of caution in the expenditure of money, but the sensualist must have a clear-headed conception of relative value. One case comes to mind regarding a patient whose biggest problem in life really was the lack of firmly held goals. He was always feeling depressed, because he felt he was drifting through life without achieving anything, but he was incapable of declaring any clear statement of just what he wanted to achieve.

His name was Louis. One day at the appointed hour he took his seat opposite my desk looking a bit sadder than usual; it was a while before he spoke a word. "I had a fight with my girl," he finally said, slumping into a state of near incommunicado. I had to drag the details out of him, even though he really did want to recapitulate the whole thing so that he could justify his own position at every point.

Louis and his girl, he told me, and I can't describe her because he never did, had gone to bed together the previous Friday night. After overcoming an initial timidity, they went at each other like hungry people finding the first restaurant in a thousand miles. Before they fell asleep they became more intimate in conversation than they had ever been before, and she expressed a desire to see some pornographic films, which he told her were available in a nearby town. He promised to go there the next day and select a couple of choice reels.

They slept, and on the Saturday morning, he drove her from her place, where they had stayed, to a store in a major city which was two hours' drive away. Louis' car wasn't the latest and greatest and on the way his fan belt broke and he had to call a garage to replace it, one of those unfortunate incidents which cost the travelling motorist about twenty dollars. He could have charged it on his gasoline credit card and saved his cash, but he was a frugal man and hated to incur installment debt.

However, by the time they arrived in the next city and had lunch, he was beginning to worry about how much was left of his paycheck. She stayed at the restaurant over coffee while he went to buy the film which was the purpose of their trip. She was excited about the prospect. An hour later, Louis came back, empty handed. She was furious; she couldn't understand his explanation, wouldn't even listen to it.

What had happened was that the film, together with the cost of renting a projector—for a week because he couldn't get back until the next Saturday—would have taken every dollar he had, and there was gasoline needed in the car, etc. He had thought of just getting the film and renting a projector when he got back to his home town and could get some more money or better rates, but by the time he got back, he figured, the rental stores would be closed. It was all very reasonable, as he explained it. On the return trip his girlfriend froze, not exchanging a word, and when he pulled up in front of her apartment, she swiftly left the car, slamming the door. He followed her but she slammed the door to her apartment and wouldn't make the slightest response to his entreaties to open the door and talk.

Poor Louis, he had squandered most of his money anyway on a fruitless trip; and now that that was gone, he had ruined what could have been an exquisite night of sexual play, just to save money. I reminded Louis that he had spent dollars quite freely in wooing this girl the week before, and that before he had met her, he had gone to the metropolis nearby and spent twenty-five dollars a crack, to use a handy phrase, for a ten minute commercial sex spree. So wherefore this sudden caution when he came to a situation which was what he had described as the kind of relationship he yearned for?

Well, it wasn't as simple as this, but Louis again had been a victim of his own disorganized thinking. It cost him a good deal more to restore the friendly situation that existed before that ruined Saturday.

Too many people operate like this. The same men, young and old, who think nothing of working and saving for months to buy a used car so that they can overcome the obstacle of limited transportation, which they think is what is keeping them from fulfilling their sexual goals, balk at some further expense of a rather paltry nature when it would be at least another step in the direction of realizing their professed aims. When this happens, the therapist of course begins to question whether their professed aim is really what they want and if it is going to be achieved. Some people continue all their lives repeating a pattern which throws up obstacles to attaining their desires, so much so that one might conclude that just *wanting*, the raw, uncomfortable feeling of desire unsatisfied, is what they want to perpetuate.

There is something else behind the problem which actually amounts to trading one insecurity for another, at least in many cases I have seen. The patient is unsure of his own performance, fearful of failure with women, terrified of the action he must take in exposing his own human nature to reach out and achieve his sexual goal, so he transfers his insecurity about money, which stems from the same basic source, and that becomes the reason for not succeeding.

If there is one basic rule that I can state with some authority, it is that there is no expense too great, no matter what it costs, to achieve sexual fulfillment. At this point some cynical readers who have dropped out of therapy with the excuse that it costs too much, even though it would have solved their sexual hangups, are going to say, "Sure, that's what all you psychologists and psychoanalysts say when you're telling people they need your help at so much an hour."

And that's true. But I also make the same statement if I am advising someone to spend a year's savings for two tension-free weeks in Hawaii with his sex partner, or if I'm telling a patient that the cost of establishing an apartment for convenient love-making is worth it considering the frustration otherwise, or if I am advising someone to undertake marriage or divorce, either of which can be terribly expensive.

Another dramatic example of the economics of sex is evident in a patient that I did *not* treat. He came to me over ten years ago on the recommendation of a mutual friend. He was a rising young executive with a good income and an excellent outlook for the future with a solid company in a small town nearby—actually it was a hundred miles, roughly. His name was Baron and he had what was not an insurmountable problem.

Baron, in order to have orgasm, had to have his sex partner perform a very special set of visual accommodations. It is some measure of his persuasiveness that he actually did find women willing to go along with his desires, which might be thought peculiar. The girl had to appear before him wearing a black lace bra, black lace panties, dark hose and garters, high-heeled shoes, and a very specific facial make-up, including long false eyelashes, and dark linings that exaggerated the size of her eyes. Her hair had to be long and wildly curled, but with every strand in place.

The girl would stand before him dressed like this and Baron would begin to get an immense erection, all the more urgent because of the rarity of finding someone who would play along with him. The lights were kept on, brightly, as Baron stripped, and, savoring her every visual flourish as she stood there, he would advance on her, aching for penetration. His masculinity was so prominent that it could never be doubted, and even the woman was usually surprised that a man who required such exotic stimulation would react in such bull-like stature.

Up until the moment he touched her, she would have to be just standing there, almost motionless, except the most feminine urging of her pubis, too gentle to be called grinding, more like a beckoning. When he reached her with his splendid organ between them, then and only then could she slide onto the bed on her back, and slowly, slowly, fold her panties down to expose her vagina. He would mount her directly but taking the utmost care not to disturb her hair, or bra, or shoes. Then and only then would he stroke his manhood into her to the hilt. Encouraged by her grimace of penetration, that necessary little ache of love which he knew she was enjoying, he would reach a roaring climax, all the while never taking his eyes off her face.

He copulated in a raised position, so that only his penis was in her; his body did not touch her stomach or breasts, or legs, just the erogenous zone itself. As he looked down on the perfectly accoutred woman, savoring the ultra-femininity of her garments and their seductive perfume, if one thing came out of place–if in her own panting reaction she flinched and a false eyelash fell loose, or if a shoe fell off or her lipstick smeared from a hand pressed to her mouth, he was rendered immediately impotent. He would lose his erection and couldn't get it back, and was furious with the woman.

Well, needless to say, the number of available, attractive women in the small town where Baron was a well-known community pillar was limited. Even more limited was the number who for some curiosity or willingness to ingratiate themselves, were willing to dress as he specifically desired. Especially after the disappointment and shock of having the pleasurable insertion deflated through some inconspicuous flaw that was inherent in the process, almost bound to happen, and then to be cursed for it as though it were their fault.

Baron did not come for treatment, not because of money, but because it would have meant sacrificing his Saturdays to make the trip to my office in the city, and that day was important to him because he used it to get ahead in his business, preparing for the coming week, earning more and more money.

As time went on, Baron, who would not trust any local therapist with his problem, gradually got a reputation in his town, from the girls who were upset with his performance and displeasure. He could find few girls to go along with him, and his temper outbursts, when they failed him by slipping from perfection, grew violent. The last I heard of him he had moved cross country to start a new life. Ten years of economic gain had gone down the drain for him when he was arrested for assault by a girl who was known to be available for money. There was a nasty civil suit threatened, a settlement trying to hush it up, and eventually he was fired anyway, drinking up much of his savings in a period of unemployment before deciding to start out afresh. I hope he started with therapy; it would have cost a lot less to start years ago and would have been a lot more satisfying. He wouldn't have demanded all those superfeminine garments and could have enjoyed placing his engorged manhood into a naked body that could be stroked and mussed and petted in passion. He could have found a lot of women for that.

To skim over Baron's problem, he was insecure about his own masculinity, which could have been overcome if he had not so inflamed it by hiding it and feeding it. The idea his unconscious pursued to solve his problem was that if the girl dressed in the manner he required she must be the ultimate of femininity. If he desired somebody so feminine, why then of course he was without a trace of doubt positively masculine, in fact the superior masculine male, wasn't he?

A well-to-do successful man answered his hotel room door during a business visit to a distant city. There stood a lovely female seeking entry. He expressed affront that she should ask a hundred dollars for her services. He slammed the door in her face. *He* won't be taken advantage of. And so, in the suite of rooms for which he was paying about $100, he retired at night and slipped his hand familiarly around his aroused penis. He had a fantasy about a lovely, clean, sophisticated, experienced call girl who came to him for a full night of pleasure and delivered a full measure of delight. He'll probably die with a bigger bank account than she will, but who'll be the bigger loser?

If you've got the money and are visiting in a distant town where you are unfamiliar with things, the only thing to fear from high-priced call girls is the possibility of vice officers watching the exchange of money. And there's little to fear along those lines, because any girl who makes $100 a night with her talented body is going to be sharp enough to keep her earning assets out of jail. She's also going to keep her body free of VD, because that would lay her up unprofitably for even longer than a prostitution rap. Hire her, let her show you every trick she's got, and if you sleep at all, when you do get up, slip a hundred dollar bill into her purse, not her hand, and smile. It will have been worth it. A little discretion covers all the possibly undesirable aspects of such commerce and the quality price generally assures trouble-free service and pride of workmanship.

Did you know that there are legitimate whorehouses in America where you can get laid by clean, regularly inspected young prostitutes who are pretty good-looking as well as being quite talented?

One such locale—and there are several—is between Reno and Las Vegas in Nevada. Millions of people have flown to Las Vegas every year for a decade and after squandering their money on the casino tables, good living and entertainment, begin to wonder if they just might top it all off with a little strange sex. But the town is a difficult one for that unless you know the ropes, and most strangers don't. There are too many willing girls with too many angles for getting more and giving less than they bargained for, even though there are some excellent, quality-conscious individual services, if you know how to find them.

The secret is, you don't look. You register in an expensive suite, something in the seventy-five to a hundred dollar a day class, and, come nightfall, there will be a rap at your door. There is only one caution necessary: She doesn't get out of your sight until the transaction is complete, and neither do your room keys, nor your valuables; just a thoughtful gesture to keep the game pure. Don't worry about police. If they knocked down your door—which they wouldn't because the hotels don't wish their clients disturbed—but if the police did and found a naked beauty in your bed, wearing nothing but toenail polish, bobbing up and down on your penis, the law would excuse itself hurriedly, apologizing profusely, and the girl wouldn't miss a stroke.

She knows. Police are looking for law-breakers, burglars especially, not for someone who is obviously gainfully employed. The whorehouses are in the counties a couple of hours' drive away from the two major gambling capitals, and anyone who qualifies as a tourist should know better than to spend a whole week in a gambling town anyway. A visit to a legal, fully authorized whorehouse is part and parcel of inspecting local color. What more delightful way to gather interesting pieces of Americana than an afternoon making the rounds of all the houses and all the girls? This isn't a travelogue, but there are bus and door-to-door air service available. One of the houses has its own airstrip. This is brought out to illustrate that no matter what excuses any person may devise, there is no excuse for not getting laid in this great, freedom-loving land of ours.

No arguments will be heard regarding expense. Not from anyone who ever bought a used car, lost his paycheck in a card game, or spent his vacation touring points of historic interest, or, worse, loafing at some so-called tourist resort where the prospects for being laid are nil because everybody's engaged in too much activity to be bothered.

Commercial sex is not really advocated unless it is something you have never tried, an expert, a professional, in which case it might be worth remembering. Generally this sort of service is only required by those who don't have the time to establish personal relationships with the girls in whom they insert their penis. Except for transitory situations this should be the exception to the rule.

When engaging in sex with prostitutes, the opportunity lies in technique and the exploration of diversity from an athletic standpoint. It must be remembered that there is no opportunity for involvement or closeness, which is a necessary facet of the ordinary human sexual encounter. It happens more often than you'd think that persons who go to prostitutes, or "Johns," as the girls call them, frequently will pay for their services without using their bodies, just to have someone to be close to, to talk to, to experience a quick off-on, adjustable involvement. Well, the girls usually go along with this arrangement, but the fact is they'd rather go to bed; it's easier work. They too are hungup in non-involvement. If a John keeps coming back for years he will never get more than a poor substitute for involvement and closeness from a whore. You pay for sex and that's what you get.

The principal reason for mentioning expense is in building up to a forthcoming prolonged discussion of things that are happening at the sex clubs which are a burgeoning, smash-success phenomenon in America. Economically, they are successful because they provide something that a lot of people want. The compleat sensuous male will find it worth his every penny to ante up the initiation fees and dues and transportation costs, even if the nearest one is a thousand miles away. It is a part of the new liberated sexual experience that is so rich and rare that if its cost was in handsful of diamonds it would be worth it. In this case, you are not buying sex. You are paying for the opportunity to give, to give yourself, and you must be willing to, eager to, again, and again, and again.

In any investment of money into sexual accessories, memberships, subscriptions, books, or other offers, always beware the come-on by shoddy advertisements, worded cagily for you to read between the lines. There are many mail-order firms operating on the principle that you will be too embarrassed to complain about not having received fair value. Sure, many are reputable, but the best practice is to write first, asking for some assurance of dependability or quality, or testimonial, before sending any considerable sum of money.

But when you do investigate some notice of sexual intrigue and still find that you are interested in the promise extended, then by all means invest, invest now! It may not be listed on the stock market, but when you're 90 years old and can't take advantage of the sexual possibilities, it just might be!

It should be repeated that whenever you encounter a situation in which money is to be spent to pave the way for achieving a sexual goal, you should not hesitate. Analyze the matter if you find yourself saying you can't afford it, lest you fall into the common trap of throwing up arbitrary economic barriers to fulfilling your sexual goals. And if you really don't have the money, even after you recognize that it is indeed worth it—and if you can't earn it—then be sure to quiz yourself as to whether or not the expenditure really is necessary for your sexual goal. Or is it an excuse, an alibi to keep you from a fearful approach to sexual involvement?

CHAPTER XI

WHEN SEX IS A PARTY

The road winds through towering eucalyptus trees in the foothills of the Santa Monica Mountains, a neighborhood of impressive homes on various acreage, obscured from the roadway by lavish tropical foliage that is the prerogative of those who can spend fifty to two hundred thousand dollars for a place to live. It is Friday night and, from the stream of cars climbing toward the most elaborate estate of them all, obviously a party night. At the end of the road, iron gates with a guard open the way to the ultimate estate, and through them all the partygoers pass. At the door of the mansion, the hosts greet each arriving couple the way it would be at any suburban gathering on a weekend night. Any stranger who walked in would think he was at a common variety party, except that no strangers can get in.

Inside the well-furnished, softly carpeted and warmly-lit rooms, couples, foursomes, and larger and smaller groups are mingling, some in the kitchen-bar area, some in the hall-like living room, others in the billiards parlor or around the outdoor fireplace on the patio at poolside. Most of the people are well dressed; but in the same way that the parking lot is packed with everything from economy Volkswagons to costly sports cars and limousine class luxury sedans, with license plates from as far away as Texas and Arizona, the people inside are mixed in appearance.

Arriving at the party, people embrace in greetings. There is laughter, an atmosphere of warmth and good humor and fun.

A men's store magnate and his showgirl wife, clad in stunning mod fashions, stand there, drinks in hand, conversing with a conservatively dressed husband-wife team of school teachers and another couple consisting of a bearded computer expert in a sports short and his wife in bell-bottom slacks. There are artists and salesmen, film studio and recording executives, writers, doctors, scientists and businessmen. And there are housewives and typists, dancers, students, waitresses, plumbers, carpenters and even a policeman.

They are talking about music, books,

people, films, television, relating personal experiences, telling jokes and laughing, just like a thousand parties that happen everywhere. The only thing they all have in common is a strong interest in sexuality. A naked blonde walks casually through the billiards room on her way upstairs, apparently bringing a drink to somebody, but apart from nonchalant appraisal of her very presentable charms, nobody takes particular notice. There are men and women swimming in the heated pool naked, but inside the socializing areas nudity is unusual.

The couples mix. Husbands and wives, boyfriends and girlfriends, do not stick together all night, separating either upon prearranged signals or by choice at some spontaneous point of socializing. Strangers walk up to strangers and introduce themselves, either singly or in couples. They are all there for the same thing, because although it might be a PTA party from the looks of the people present, this is a sex club.

At some point of the evening, mutually appreciative couples who have just met pair off and leave the group, seeking out an empty bedroom. They undress and make love. Later they rejoin their own wives and husbands, girlfriends and boyfriends, or seek out other new people to meet. The conversational line that brings any man and woman to the point that they may decide to communicate sexually, is "Do you want to swing?" There is no obligation or indirect coercion to "swing" with any individual or at all. It is all a matter of choice for the people involved, without "swapping" of partners or any involuntary aspect. Those who don't care to swing can play pool, drink and talk, watch television, listen to music, dance, swim or play games, never disturbed by the sexual activities taking place in the private areas of the mansion. In fact, by special arrangement, there have been times that out-of-town guests came to these parties, held every Friday and Saturday night of the week, and went home praising the party in general and the people they had met, but never discovering the sexual nature of the gathering.

This is only one of a dozen sex or "swinging" clubs that abound in the Los Angeles area. One is an elaborate, former millionaire's estate situated in the forested hills overlooking the Pacific. Another is a mountain lodge style clubhouse. There is one in the rural area beyond the suburbs and another operates out of a large suite in an apartment building. The sex clubs are experiencing a tremendous growth because we are living in a fast-moving, rapidly changing society; people are realizing that we must continue to grow as humans if we are to prosper and be healthy. The sex clubs bring together people who believe that individuals should be free to do whatever they want with their bodies and minds as long as they do not infringe on the rights of others or break any laws. All of them are rigidly against drugs for this reason.

Some clubs have no central gathering place but operate an office where congenial couples can be introduced to each other, or singles to singles, with the idea that they will go out to dinner together, or for drinks, or anywhere they might get to know one another better, and perhaps later go to bed together if so inclined. There are night clubs where it is generally known that the couples visiting there on certain nights wish to pair up with other couples and repair to a motel or private home for sexual purposes if they strike up a mutual desire.

The club described in the opening of this chapter is an ideal one for those who are known as "rookie" swingers or newcomers. With a membership of over two hundred couples, about half of them attending the two weekly parties, the club is open only to husbands and wives or lover twosomes. Called 101, the organization has brought together many of the ideal ingredients for successful sensual experiences. They offer excitement and relaxation; they have an articulated philosophy, a stimulating set of physical surroundings, sensual people, a comfortable style and even an effective information system, a weekly bulletin.

Among the club's stated doctrines is a dedication to strengthening and beautifying the private relationship between men and women who love one another. Swinging is considered a sharing experience, and as such, is an expression of a couple's mutual love for one another and respect for their individuality. The men and women, whether married or just dating, suspend by mutual agreement the exclusive right to each other's bodies for the period of the parties. They do not cheat on one another; in fact, any clandestine meeting of unmarried members outside of the club is grounds for dismissal. The club represents total acceptance of the concept that personal sexual freedom is every individual's right and that it is an act of the greatest love, and greatest personal strength, to grant temporary freedom to someone you love in a way that will not damage your own relationship. States the club's operator, "You still have a primary responsibility to your marriage or your lover, and any time swinging interferes with that responsibility you should drop it."

Some people of conventional backgrounds will surely debate that couples who could share their husbands or wives with others couldn't really love one another. But love feeds on love, and reaches out. Jealousy, bondage of the human spirit, and self-deception are damaging. These couples are not deceiving one another with secret dalliances that would break up their marriage if discovered. Both the women and men learn to experience the reality that they can be attractive and attracted to other people, a truth to which statistics on marital discord attest. Such couples allow one another to step into a world of sensual freedom; as a result their marriage is reinforced, because they have experienced extra-marital sex and still return by choice to the love of their partners. In fact, most swingers close out their night by going to bed with one another and expressing that love with all the openness and eagerness of free choice. Freedom can be wonderful and sometimes the compunction of the marriage contract can be a dampening force.

As mentioned, there are a variety of such clubs, including a number for single men and women, and with different facilities and styles. Some of them do practice social nudity, with most people doffing all their clothes shortly after entering, but usually if a person is more comfortable with some or all of their clothes on, there is no pressure to make them conform. In some clubs couples will engage in sex in front of others, but in most of them at least some degree of privacy is provided for love-making. All of the clubs are supported by dues. For example, the club described at length charges a $100 initiation fee plus $20 a month. This, however, is not the sole criterion for admission.

A personal interview of each couple is carried out at a location other than the secret party mansion. Interested couples are given a chance to ask questions and find out the rules and policies of the club. In addition, the club screens its membership on several categories of personal appearance, attitudes, and social acceptability. People who are disturbed, or drink too much, or take drugs, or do not take care of their appearance, cannot gain admission for ten times the fee, even though some have tried.

Not all clubs are so strict in their screening as the 101 group, however, some of them operating on the principle that people who have behavior problems or lack physical perfection will tend to match up with one another while the beautiful people seek one another out. Of course, the only way this approach can work is when there is completely voluntary participation. No girl should be forced to go with any man, either by pre-agreements or coercive party games. Even in the privacy of the bed—if this condition exists—it must still be the woman's choice to decide on her sexual practices and set the limits of her own participation. Otherwise the purpose of such sexual adventure is lost.

Ideally in a sex club, a girl should be able to go to a bedroom with a man and, if he does not arouse her, or himself is not aroused, they should be able to return to the social areas without personal reactions of anger, resentment or, worst of all, crushed egos. This does happen. Men and women who have had fantastic sex experiences together will greet one another with embraces and kisses and warmest inquiries into each other's lives. Whatever happens, they *have* done something together; they've been human together.

Often a "rookie" husband will fear for his wife or a wife for her own person, since once she goes off with a man who seems to present himself in a positive, friendly way, the pursuit of sex might drive him to violence if she did not perform as he wished her to. The possibility has been considered; that is why there are seldom locks on doors, or isolated bedrooms, and why there is always a stern warning that rough behavior is grounds for immediate ouster. Women have told me of certain clubs where a girl no sooner enters the front door that someone seizes her, strips her and drags her to a room full of other bodies. But even in these cases, a woman who protests loudly enough is turned loose with curses.

Couples—especially newcomers to the scene—should investigate carefully before getting involved, because any scene where personal liberty is placed in jeopardy defeats the only possible reason for joining in the first place. There are people who no amount of sexual freedom will free, because they are still acting on antiquated notions that equate sex and women with dirt, gruffness, and an absence of gentleness. Their ideas of free sex come straight from the old "smokers" of yesteryear where it was traditional that, since every other "evil" like cards, gambling and drinking already was being engaged in, sex movies or prostitutes certainly ought to join in. Obviously, this kind of libertarianism is every bit as puritanical as the pilgrims'.

The 101 club, which has such ideal conditions for beginners that people have joined from a thousand miles away, coming only on vacations, tries to maintain an excitement like any party host. There is the big living room which serves as the center for socializing, and there is a room in Tahitian decor, and a nonverbal room with loud music for dancing and sofas for listening. Members by the way, voluntarily did much of the decorating. For sex purposes, there is one room done in psychedelic fashion; a large bedroom arranged with the exotic, veil-like partitions of a seraglio or harem; there is a waterbed room; an orgy room which consists merely of soft lights and a wall-to-wall mattress, and there are very plain and ordinary suburban type bedroom.s Couples enjoy each other sexually, splash in the shower afterward—there are ten bathrooms—and often go for a reviving swim in the ninety-degree pool. Or they dress and return to the living room and/or their spouses.

Just to enter that party scene takes courage on the part of a man. First of all, it is a fantasy world where all things are as they probably should be. There are dozens of exciting women scattered around the house, seeking the pleasure of a man who will be good to them in bed. It is a great ego trip, for each person actually is there to please himself, to enjoy others and prove nothing. The man who fears comparisons—will the girls say he is not as good in bed as somebody else, or will his mate find somebody else who is more exciting to her sexually?—probably will not succeed, for having one's ego solidly intact is practically a necessity for participation.

One male member told me that he could forecast his performance on any given night by playing a game of pool first. He had a natural talent for pool, but if he started out the night with a game and saw that he was miscueing left and right, missing shots that should have been child's play for him, then he knew he had some mental hangup that was going to constrict his sexual activity with strangers. On the other hand, when without a second look he could smash pool shot after shot with thudding accuracy into the pockets, then he knew he was in for a great night with the ladies. Nor did the symbolism of the pool cue and balls escape him.

Actually, the scene is like that of any nightclub or private party as regards one's opportunities for sexual expression, the major difference being that all of the worries about "does she or doesn't she" have been eliminated. It's all up to you. After you get over your initial shock of accepting that you now have the opportunity to turn your sexual fantasies into reality, and that every person on the premises is directed toward the same goal, it becomes like a child's trip to the candy store where a thousand different delights are visible and awaiting selection. What will they taste like?

Now comes the test of your personality, stripped of its defenses. Every girl you meet will not have to trifle with the social question, does he really want me to go to bed with him, now?—that much is known. It does not matter if you are rich or poor, tall or short, softspoken or aggressively vocal, but it does matter how you are able to convey your sensuality. The girl, by her mere presence, indicates a willingness to engage in love-making, but it is up to the individual man to communicate to her that perhaps you are the one to share herself and her experiences with tonight.

Some men are so tuned in and turned on their first night at one of the sex club parties that they can go all night long with numerous different women. Others, because of the strangeness of the whole scene or some individual body, and the imbued notion that making love to another woman is evil, either fail to perform at all or perform poorly. This experience usually is overcome quickly, however, and most of the swingers are sympathetic to the trepidations and other problems of the newcomers.

It must be realized that reality is not completely suspended. You meet girls who are having their periods. You meet girls who have an agreement with their husbands that they will not pair off until their mate does. You meet girls with hangups about astrology, or who prefer beardless men, or tall men. You meet girls who don't like to be rushed, and girls who do. You meet girls who have already enjoyed sex twice that night and really have to be encouraged to go again, expecially if their experience was not satisfying. Some girls like to go from man to man all night, counting them, and if you get her at a peak of arousal, fine, otherwise you're just an encounter en route to the sexual "high" she is seeking. Each girl, and each man, is out for his or her own sexual enjoyment, which is fair enough.

Certain husbands and wives will sit together until a couple or a man joins them. They have a pre-arranged signal. If the wife asks for a drink shortly, then the husband knows she is interested enough in the other male, so he either disappears and seeks out a female on his own, or if it's a case of a couple and he like the girl, he brings back the drink and engages the woman in a separate conversation. There are many games played. A girl who met an interesting man the week before, but had already participated sexually to the point of exhaustion, may reject several approaches early the next week, keeping her eyes open for the arrival of that certain person. Rejections are seldom hard to take. A girl who for some reason does not want to go to bed with you excuses herself to go for a drink, or to the bathroom, and looks for someone else along the way to detain her.

Privacy is not always perfect. A single room may contain two beds separated only by a thin film of curtain, with both beds occupied. A large room may be divided into several niches, with little cubicles containing a mattress and separated only by the darkness and curtains from the others. Sometimes newcomers find it difficult to perform freely under those circumstances and must wait for one of the really private locales.

Sometimes the experience is spoiled by proximity. One male told me of really getting a lovely brunette turned on, until, who should occupy the next bed but a man and a woman, the man being recognizable as her husband, so that she was reluctant to become over-enthusiastic or perform fellatio, since she feared he would recognize her and not approve.

Often a male cannot perform if he should have the poor luck to distinguish the panting voice or body of his own mate making love to somebody else nearby. Most novices must swing separately from their partners until they can come to reject their life-long conditioning and accept the reality of their mate's existence as a sexual being, and the reality of the fact that she is probably, at the same moment he is enjoying sex, enjoying the act with some other man. Other people enjoy having their partner in view and find it a real turn on.

There are a million fantasies to be lived, but reality always intrudes, sooner or later. One man told me about an experience one night in which he spent thrilling hours with one woman, going at her again and again with the woman rising to the new approach every time, as though her usual sexual expression had been limited to a single, on-and-off event.

Their fantastic love-making session was interrupted at three o'clock in the morning, however, by an irate knock on their door and her husband shouting that he had been waiting for two hours and it was time to go home. In such cases, the wife can explain, "We've just been talking—talking about a very interesting subject."

So reality continues. You and your spouse or lover are not going to simultaneously enjoy sexual experiences of similar intensity. One may have a good night while the other does not, factors which exert extreme pressures on tender egos, a condition which of itself limits the membership of such clubs. There are too few who dare. Most would like to, like to dare to, and many would like to try it once, or at least admit they are intrigued by it.

There are also several night clubs which have become known as gathering places for "swingers," often varying from night to night as to whether it is singles night or couples night. These clubs, the cocktail lounge type and the private organizations, generally, although not exclusively, restrict their advertising to underground-type newspapers, which also afford numerous want ad opportunities for like-minded couples to meet for purposes of broadening their sex lives. Better to make your couples contacts through the clubs, where you can meet the people in person, since Uncle Sam has been known to tamper with the mails in certain jurisdictions.

In the clubs, which have their own attorneys who have ruled that no law is being broken since there is no conspiracy of sex, just a gathering during which sexual pairings voluntarily occur, no raid has ever taken place or, for that matter, even threatened. At one club one night, two policemen showed up at the door, and were admitted into the hallway where they could see a party in progress and women in various states of undress, but they were there only because a backyard loudspeaker was blaring music too loudly. The officers, who volunteered that they didn't think the music was really too high in volume, were very apologetic about the intrusion and thanked the host for recognizing that they had to do their duty. He forgave them and they never came back.

In any event, from the night clubs or from personal contact at the private clubs, one often gets invited to informal parties of swingers at their own residences, and there are many of these. Some homes are practically an open house for swingers all weekend long. In the private residential gatherings, when one accepts a party invitation, there is only one difference from the general unspoken rules. Of course, as hosts, the couple inviting the others sets the decor and style of dress for the evening like at any party, but at a swinging party, accepting an invitation includes the understanding that the invited are *willing* to swing with their hosts, even though it would be a practical impossibility for the hosts to make it with *all* their guests on any given night, or even half.

If you are curious enough about the sex clubs, public and private, to investigate the phenomenon on a personal level, then consult your nearest underground newspaper.

One final caution should be reiterated regarding sex clubs. The matter of sex is fun, and in these matters, mass fun, but married couples and lovers who go to such clubs had better be sure that they do indeed love one another, understand one another and trust one another before joining. If you do not, the pressures of such activity on your ego and your mate's probably will cause anything unspokenly wrong with your alliance to surface and perhaps destroy your relationship. Such a club is the last place in the world to go to solve sexual problems or a lack of sexual harmony between you and your partner. It is a place for sexual adventure beyond the limits of you and she, and only then for the very brave people with intact egos.

CHAPTER XII

WHAT TO DO UNTIL THE ORGASM COMES

The human female consists of a biological urge surrounded by the mechanisms and implements for carrying it out. This is not to be interpreted as a degrading evaluation by any means; in fact, it is a tribute to the remarkable efficiency of the organism that there is one singular function to which it can devote such total physical employment that even the mind can be sidelined into semi-consciousness at the extremes of sexual convulsion. Nor is this physical appraisal a denial that the woman exists first as a person. Any male who tries to deny it does so at his own peril, for he who refuses to recognize the humanity and box office ticket-taking capacity of a creature in whom he intends to ejaculate, not only won't get into her anyway, but belongs in a bathroom or barnyard instead.

While there is no single push-button

turn-on for the love-making warmth of all women, there are methods of bringing about optimum performance in bed, starting from the doorway.

Certain basic assumptions must be made to delineate the joyful process of worship at the fuzzy triangle. Neither clinical charts and diagrams, nor step-by-step medical dictionary procedures will be found here. You take to the bedroom everything you need to be armed with, and the girl is going to give you a very funny look if you climb into bed with an armful of charts and maps: "Let's see, male inserts second or third digit of left extremity between ridges of (see diagram) vulva, of prostrate female in modified foetal position, etc." So the first of our basic assumptions is that you and your partner recognize that such items are useless in the bedroom; textbooks are uncomfortable as body props, and even the most tightly rolled diagram is unserviceable as a dildo.

Second, we assume that the male reader knows how to attain an erection, or is closely enough acquainted with some person or book to solicit assistance. Third, the rudiments of female anatomy should have been mastered at this point, without need of referring to breast A and breast B, such information being available in any Victorian Era marriage manual, or, for that matter, your neighborhood alley.

So, you are in proximity to a comfortable horizontal surface with a hard-on, and with you is a girl, a creature which the press is fond of calling a member of the "distaff" set, which means that she does not have a penis, and is also a good indication that you are normal. Love her you must, however fleetingly. She is beautiful, after all, not only for having all those fleshy goodies to accommodate you, but because she has spent at least sixteen long years in maturing all this lovely sex equipment. Despite all social pressures and "learning" processes devoted to stifling any inclination to use that sex equipment for anything more functional than going to the bathroom and holding up strapless dresses, her heart and hormones prevailed and she now stands ready to use her body as if she owned it, to give pleasure to herself and you. And what are you going to do with all that love if you don't put yourself inside her?

You are to her, no matter what her previous experience, equally something of a mystery, possessing the round warm projection that for much of her life was a curiosity to her, in the same way that all your masculine activities and interests were strange to her. You are the riding knight with lance, the hunter with a gun, the baseball player swinging a bat. For every projection on the front of each of you, the other has an absence every bit as appealing. The light in the room, even limited light, is important in letting one another savor these differences in the act of disrobing. Or in darkness they can be appreciated by touch. The female reflex of raising a knee or thigh to the male crotch is not a protective one; it is an act of discovery, an acknowledgment of man's pride.

The words you use at this point, to tell this woman how spectacular she is, in body warmth, in eager lips, in the bigness of her breasts, in the invitingness of her moist pubic area, the roundness of her curves in beauty of figure, or merely in the sensitivity she has to your touch, are the most important vocal contribution that can be paid in the entire process of love-making. What you say can set her free to be warmer, intensify her feeling for you, relax her tensions and magnify her anticipation. Your early caresses cover her body, stroking her neck and shoulder and following the curve of her spine, measuring the mound above her ass and cuddling the generous divisions of flesh below. Her breasts, the cleft between her waist and the jutting of her hips, the sweeping arc of her outer thigh, and the so soft whiteness of the inner thigh. And if you dwell only on our lesson in female appreciation, you do it for her as well as yourself, increasing your knowledge of her and desire to be inside her, confident that your very different male body is being measured with equal awareness by her.

As your hands chase over her body, you watch for little signals, to see if she moves her flesh to retain a certain touch, or sighs at it, or pulls from it. Her entire body offers erogenous points of interest and each girl may have her special ones—a kiss on the side of the neck, a nibble at her ear, a hand cupping a breast or lips brushing the nipples to make them stand up. Move your penis to where she can reach it or touch it with her body if she wishes, but be firm in resisting too much manual manipulation that will cost more pleasurable strokes later. Once I knew a girl who could come from the effects of a strong kiss on her buttocks, perhaps an emotional reaction, but there are strong sexual influences there.

In the same way that the clinical charts point out the lines connecting the nipples to her sex, there are vital links from buttocks to clitoris. Where a touch causes her to flex her ass muscle, it moves the clitoris itself, and you can make a quick two-handed test of that reaction. Even if she doesn't haunch up her fanny, just mauling the flesh upward does the trick. Gentle fingers alongside, rather than atop, are best for setting the clitoris to throbs, and if you run back and forth, digitally speaking, clitoris to vagina, spreading the wetness, she'll soon move with you. When this plateau is reached, she is ready for entry–if she wasn't before you started all the fooling around with her body.

Using any or all the tactics suggested for prolonging the heady feeling of uniting, like alternating current, penetrating her like advancing waves on a beach, you struggle to put yourself inside this person. The symbolism is pyrotechnic. In all our lives, which start inside another person, we are never allowed to really place ourselves outside ourselves again, except in this thrilling see-saw which is closest, the woman containing a body's most urgent member and the man penetrating, churning, thrusting, until with an ache from toes to hairline he spills part of himself there, as his partner convulses her most vital part as in the onset of birth. She lives, doing what she was made for, and you live inside her, giving her that convulsion called orgasm.

You strive for simultaneous orgasm, but is it really necessary? Sometimes a hangup over feeling that this is a must, a signpost, an applause, and perhaps the only indication of success, can spoil the fun of lovemaking by imposing arbitrary demands in a situation that must be flexible. Although simultaneous orgasm is desirable, the lack of it is no sign of failure, unless the participants regard it so. Who's keeping score? Especially in case of personal tension, it can be a matter of the utmost thrill to completely forego the touch-down syndrome of he-and-she gang-bang climaxes and pursue an unlimited chain of alternates instead–you doing it to her, then she to you, then you to her, and then, perhaps, starting from a higher plateau with renewed zest, then the struggle for double come.

Depending on the level of your intimacy, if you set out from the first touch of bodies to try to achieve simultaneous climax, and do, then both have succeeded and, being weary, may sleep or seek pleasure elsewhere. You've done what you set out to do, so it's over, and you're missing a lot of sex play. But if you begin by sliding your tongue into her crotch and licking down to her vagina until she begins to rock her whole lower body and comes in your mouth, then it's your turn. She applies her lips to your penis, her tongue too, and takes it inside her mouth, sucking and French kissing it and gliding up and down on the moveable flesh until you set off a fountain of semen in her.

It's your turn again, and you can tease her with your hands or penetrate her vagina with a dildo or vibrator, or lick or digitally stimulate her anus, her breasts, until her body is afire with ridges of heat and her vulva is blood red and ticking off the seconds, pumping. Then she climbs on you, for insertion or play, and you've begun again. The glory of alternating orgasms is not only the special, undivided devotion that can be paid, but, as each partner takes his turn stimulating the other, the act arouses again the person performing, readying him for the next turn. When you do finally get to simultaneous orgasm, it'll not only be synchronized, it'll be a body earthquake.

The alternation procedure is specially good for the male ego, since although he would find difficulty in going right into a second love-making session after depleting himself in the first lusty orgasm, he can re-arouse time and again with the delays of rotating love. And at each turn you praise the extraordinary skill and ardor of your partner, elevating her and exciting her to greater performance on the next round.

If the whole procedure of love-making is unspecific, it is because it should be. It should be a matter of feeling. You are together at a love-feast, and you choose your own courses from the menu, letting your sensuality be your guide. There are no set rules. Some couples find the greatest pleasure in seating themselves in Indian style and embracing, naked, legs around one another's waist. With the man inserting himself fully, neither of them move a muscle from that moment, if possible, until the frenzied climax of tension and awareness. Others fly at one another and lock genitals on the run, midway in the bedroom, thrashing and rolling and bouncing and grappling and exploding. Some couples unite and come without exchanging a word and others are exclaiming and moaning like revivalists in the ecstasy of salvation.

In the bedroom you must do what you feel, once you know what you feel and can trust it. Following your feelings, showing them and acting on them, will create the greatest tolerable pleasure within both of your capacities. That is creative sex.

CHAPTER XIII

VARIETIES OF SEXUAL MOTION

One night I received a frantic telephone call from a close friend whose boyfriend was in a desperate condition and needed help immediately, or so she said. Trying to be helpful, I went to her apartment, a very informal, mod-type pad which she and the boyfriend were sharing, and she immediately rushed me to him. He was in the bathroom. He was sitting on the toilet. Not being a specialist in this particular area, I tried to summon up some sort of professional approach, unaccustomed as I am to practicing in the bathroom, and said, "Er—what seems to be the trouble?"

He confided that he was stuck there, a position which he described with such earnestness and "spaced-out" verbalization that it was evident he was on a trip, probably LSD. He couldn't get up, he insisted, because the toilet bowl was sucking him down, trying to swallow his entire person. He was sure that the relentless suction was going to pull him in and he would disappear in a gurgling flush when his resistance gave out, drowning somewhere deep in the apartment building's plumbing. I could see that his imagination and self-assessment were suffering, but being neither plumber nor marine rescue expert, there was little I could do except console the girlfriend and tell her that it would all wear off when the LSD did, which was the way it turned out, twenty-four hours later, leaving more of a scar on his rump than his memory.

The only lesson we can draw from the experience, aside from the obvious one about steering clear of LSD, is that the position in which we do things can be very important to our enjoyment of them. This is especially so when it comes to sex, for the true sensualist will want to try every possible position that occurs to the imagination and can be performed by some contortion of the human body.

Another point comes to mind. I happened to be physically communicating with a luscious brunette one evening—and she had been quite passive about it all up to the point of insertion. I had fondled her breasts and stripped her and fondled her breasts and toyed with her sex and removed her panties and toyed with her sex, and while she didn't object to the proceedings, she was not howling with delight about it. But at the moment I lay her back on the mattress and entered her she began squirming, yelping and emitting little cries which encouraged me to continue banging away, fully assured that my technique was driving her wild with ecstasy. Alas, it turned out that I had bedded her on the one spot in the mattress where a coiled wire spring had broken through the surface, and this iron prod was stabbing her posterior painfully. So what I had interpreted as a passionate response to my sexual skill was merely a case of acute discomfort.

Some anatomy majors have recorded, with full diagrams, a total of one hundred and twelve sexual positions—although I personally can only picture about ninety-nine in my mind at this moment—so there are enough variations to diversify the relationship of any two people. But if you're going to test them all, remember the prime goal of it all is pleasure, and pleasure does require a certain measure of comfort.

A tall, well-built athletic type I know boasts that he really gives the girls a thrill by picking them up, legs to the ceiling, and licking their crotch; he hugs the girl's waist while she dangles downward and nibbles at his penis. Even if the woman weighs one hundred and twenty-five, he says, it is easy because she naturally bends her knees one on each shoulder, which supports a good deal of her weight. Well, I can see that for about thirty seconds for the unusualness of it all, but after that I'd tend to drop it. I believe the woman should be comfortable, and the man needs his strength.

There is also the vital factor of personal preference. Until the female indicates an enthusiasm for one of those complex variations that sometimes seem to imitate copulating lobsters, with limbs every which way, the sensuous male thoughtfully lets her select her ease, secure in the knowledge that the comfortable lay is the best lay.

A friend of mine who owns a water bed has had a virtual parade of women in it, all of them eager to try out something new. A water bed is precisely that. Used in the bedroom, and rather inexpensive, too, they consist of a watertight, plastic sealed mattress literally floating on an enclosure of water instead of box springs. There is a curious weightless feeling when lying on it. You really are afloat. You sink into the mattress; it pushes back at you and even rocks you with gentle waves.

After a steady stream of conquests aboard this water bed, however, my friend ran into trouble one night. The girl seemed reluctant at first but assented, apparently more interested in love-making than in the unusualness of the bed. They were in the process of making love when, with sudden terror, the girl withdrew from under him, twisted away and sped for the bathroom, hand to her mouth. It seems she was the type who is so subject to seasickness that she can't take the ferry or ride a canoe in the park. It was quite a shock to the fellows's ego to have the girl telling him by her actions that his sexual attentions were making her sick, but possibly it was only the water bed.

Don't make waves, or at least, before you rig a velvet-padded swing in your bedroom, or attach stirrups to the chandelier, remember the basic positions of love-making are the best for general use. In fact, that's how they became the basics, because they are the most used, most popular, most successful, and most comfortable.

Social scientists are able to predict the style of love-making that you are likely to engage in by knowing your socio-economic status. In general, males of the lower classes utilize only the traditional positions with their wives and consider any variation of the basic positions perverse. And the lower-class socio-economic male often is not concerned about the female reaching a climax, but only on his reaching it. There has been some speculation as to why the female permits this to occur, and it is possible that she has been so defeated in life's struggles that she has lost the desire to compete or assert herself in the sphere of living. Otherwise she engages in a popular female sport known as cheating.

Middle socio-economic individuals will try novelty in love-making but insist on privacy and usually frown on group sexual activities. For many people this outlook is fine, since plenty of variety is possible between any couple in a private situation.

The upper socio-economic class individuals have no limitations in their sexual activities and try to experience all varieties of love-making, which is another reason besides money for trying to break into the upper classes. What is bread for the lower classes becomes steak for the middle classes and, for the upper classes, it's gourmet dining.

Whatever your background, when you unzip your fly you are faced with five basic varieties of love-making: traditional, positional, oral, anal and combined. The traditional or missionary position is that in which intercourse occurs with the female lying on her back, legs spread open, with the male on top with his face facing hers. No further details will be given about it. I have observed that even in the case of inmates in institutions for the mentally retarded, with IQ levels hovering at about fifteen (or so low that they can barely learn how to feed themselves) the boys and girls manage enough imagination to copulate with one another, usually discovering the missionary position. In fact they are even clever enough to deceive attendants who are always watching out for this sort of thing.

I remember one instance in which a boy and girl in their chronological and physical teens, but otherwise children, dug a hole in the front lawn, covered it up with a green blanket, and had several other inmates stand around the hole to hide it while they locked in sex inside.

In many states the traditional or missionary position is the only way a person may engage in sex legally, including with his own wife. The missionary position, by the way, got its slightly derisive name from religious teachers who practiced sex in the dark, the woman lying back and opening her legs in full sacrificial knowledge that despite the nastiness of it all, it was God's will and the only way to procreate new members of the congregation. Some states have written this code into the law so that even a married couple could be sentenced to a long jail term for any variation, or, as the moralists would say, deviation. Fortunately the legal authorities are reluctant to prosecute under these statutes as it is difficult to find adequate witnesses in most cases. Thankfully, for sanity's sake, most states are now clearing up their outmoded laws and by the twenty-first century this madness may cease. Meanwhile, in most states of the union, if you lick your wife's sex you are a lawbreaker, a fugitive from justice and an embezzler of sexual goodies and ought to be behind bars. Just because you've been getting away with it, don't feel too safe. There actually are cases of people sentenced to prison for putting their penis in their wife's anus, or in some other legally improper orifice.

Positional sex is a pleasant variant on the traditional and its only limitation is the physical condition of the participants, which is a good reason for trying to keep in top shape. Some of the more common diversional positions for intercourse are:

1. Female sits in chair, legs apart, and man straddles her as he sits facing her. It doesn't matter if the chair is upholstered or not, but I wouldn't recommend it on a park bench with splintered slate and protruding nails.

2. Female lies face down on bed and male gets on top of her and inserts penis in vagina, or sometimes, the anus.

3. Female lies on her side and male on his side, fitting himself like an armchair to her, inserting his penis into vagina or anus.

4. Female lies on edge of bed so that her legs are clear; she can be either facing down or up. Male standing at edge of bed grips her legs, one on each side of his body and inserts penis in vagina. Anal intercourse also is possible in these positions but is not as comfortable for the female as either 2 or 3.

5. Female lies on her back, facing male. Male inserts penis as in the traditional position, but then, instead of humping her with just the usual up and down movements of his body, he turns slowly clockwise and continues to turn as far as he can. Usually an orgasm is reached before their bodies are shaped like a cross. With practice a male should be able to tick all the way around so that his toes are opposite the female's head. Also works counterclockwise, in case you're left-handed.

6. Male lies down, legs outstretched, face upward. Female, facing him, sits on top of him, inserting penis into vagina. This is one of the few positions in which the male is able to view the female's body while engaging in intercourse. It also prolongs the sex act because the seminal fluid must travel upward before he can have an orgasm. However, since he can also suck her nipples in this position,

that factor speeds up the orgasm.

7. Female gets on her knees and male inserts penis from the rear. The position is probably the best for deepest penetration of the female. It is sometimes called "dog style."

8. Male lies on his back, face upward. Female sits on him, facing away from him while he is inserting penis. Both the male and female can draw up their legs to vary this position, and penetration is very deep.

9. Female lies on her back, or in missionary position and male is on top, facing her, but instead of having the female's legs flat, he brings her legs up against her chest and continues to pump in this position.

10. Many of these positions can be varied by doing them in a standing position. Try them out in the shower, where it can be very sensual, even lathering up each other.

There are scorcs of variations possible from these basic positions by varying the angle of legs, the arch of the body or the direction of entry. Ask what she wants and don't be afraid to ask for what you want to try. If she wants to spread her legs, bend over and grip the edge of the bathtub while you penetrate from the rear, try it. If you would like to do it "dog style" only with her standing on her head, or if you wonder what it would be like to try missionary style, modified by placing her feet around your neck, on the coffee table, why not, as long as she agrees and the coffee table is sturdy enough? The only limit on positional sex is that it should not be injurious to either party. Any position that you can accomplish physically that is satisfying should be used. Keep in mind that if a muscle is not used, it atrophies and dies.

One of the greatest experiences you can have is oral love-making. It is interesting to note that the most successful prostitutes have learned this and usually find that males want them to perform oral copulation, or fellatio. Some people consider it dirty and disgusting since the genitals are going double duty as organs of elimination. But according to actual microscopic examination of slides, the only thing dirty about oral sex is that the *mouth* does contain a great many varieties of bacteria which may be transferred to the less populated genitals. However, since it usually happens that the persons thus engaged have previously had mouth-to-mouth contact, they already share the same bacteria colonies.

Just as intercourse is varied by the different positions, oral sex also has many variations. The truly sensual male will want to experience as many as he can perform. Some females are able to make love to a male most effectively by showing their affection for his penis and striving to bring him to a climax in their mouth. They savor his taste and try to experience another way of having something of him in them. The male who can effectively perform cunnilingus is fast on the way to becoming a true epicurean of sex and can experience many lovely taste thrills.

To inspire your female to perform oral delights on your behalf, learn to bring her to ecstasy with your tongue and lips in her crotch. The sixty-nine position, with your head at her crotch and her head at your crotch, permits simultaneous oral copulation. Either partner can be on top, or it can be done lying sideways or, as we mentioned briefly before, standing up, with some exertion. Part her legs and her vulva and bury your tongue against her clitoris, licking it gently and sucking it toward you. Run your tongue into her, back and forth, and suck, and when you have found the specific little movement that excites her most, she will tell you by moving her body to the tune of it. It is like setting a fire in her and the male who learns to appreciate the feel of a woman having an orgasm in his mouth is really beginning to get down to it, the heart of sexuality.

A great sensation for the free male is called "around the world," which he can perform on a female but cannot be truly appreciated until it is received. The female slowly licks every part of his anatomy, and I mean every part. She starts with his forehead, eyes, cheeks, chin, neck, shoulders, arms, fingers, chest, stomach, toes, legs, chest, thighs, back, buttocks and anus, and by the time she arrives from this journey and reaches his testicles and penis, he is standing at attention to greet her, and ready to come.

Application of the female tongue and

the sucking motion of a woman's lips on a man's penis are among the greatest pleasures in store for the sensuous male. If you are lying on your side she can suck both your penis and testicles. If she holds the top of the penis with her hand and continuously licks the shaft and the testicles you will feel your sex hormones rise. After she caresses the rim around the head of the penis and licks the center hole, you can shift positions and have her lie on her back. You straddle her body with your legs and you place your penis in her mouth while she holds the testicles in the palm of her hand. As you hold her head move your penis forward and backward in her mouth until you reach orgasm. It feels like the earth left its axis.

None of the foregoing is a map of sexual paradise to be followed like a guidebook. Such a step-by-step procedure would defy the basic nature of sensuality. In bed there are two of you and the male must feel free to act and to be acted upon in an experience that is the ultimate in sharing. Let your feelings go and let them direct your actions, while always trying to anticipate what your partner's feelings and desires are, fulfilling them at every turn. If you can't guess them by the look in her eye, the changes in her breathing, the movement of her body, and if she doesn't grab your penis and direct it, or seize the initiative herself, then try anything, try everything. When you're exhausted and your imagination is depleted, too, you could always use words.

CHAPTER XIV

ARTIFICIAL WAYS TO LIVEN UP SEX

William J., a successful young businessman, drives a big yellow Cadillac around Los Angeles. He drives down the busy shopping areas of Hollywood, through the decp canyon roads, and along the highway to the beaches. Having attained great enough wealth to last the rest of his life, William can afford to do a lot of anything he likes. He can fulfill all his dreams. And so he drives a lot. It is a big automobile, with all the extra touches possible, but you rarely see a girl at his side. The reason you don't see the girl at his side is because William J. believes in acting out his fantasies. The girl is in his lap, "eating" him as he drives. The fantasy is a curious one, and from my experience as a listener, a quite common one, although not every male gets to carry it out.

The implications and the elements are interesting. First of all, there is the vehicle, a complex machine which most men relate to as the controller. There are few situations in the highly specialized world today in which a single person is so clearly in charge. He is the operator, able to choose the direction, the speed, the maneuvers of a large mechanism that encloses him womb-like. Yet he functions as the brain, the guiding force, almost anonymously in traffic situations. The driver can choose the entertainment as he proceeds, the radio or stereo music, and he can choose to compete with other vehicles if he wishes. There is a purr, a slight vibration from a powerful motor in an excellently built automobile, and it can jostle the seat slightly, enough to provoke sexual fantasy. What a delicious position to have all those buttons to push, all those levers and gears to manipulate, and to have the contrast in your lap of living, warm lips performing the ultimate oral service, while your attention, necessarily diverted, tends to delay and heighten the orgasm.

Whatever meaning the fantasy may have will vary slightly from man to man, depending on his relationship to machines as much as his feelings toward women. But one factor which is decidedly a contribution to the mind-blowing excitement is the daring of practically carrying out in public the most intimate of sexual acts, unknown to those you are driving by. This fantasy would not be recommended by the National Safety Council, however, since there have been no tests made to determine whether or not a motorist is able to be in complete control of his vehicle, or whether his alertness and driving ability are dangerously reduced during the phase of sexual excitement and orgasm. Can you keep your feet off the pedals? Come to think of it, if you were ever stopped by a cop, just what sort of a ticket would the flustered civil servant write out? Suspect driving under the influence of moist, hot lips. Girl passenger had odor of *man* on her breath. . . .

Being a believer in law and order to a certain extent, as long as it does not trample upon personal desire, I cannot recommend this particular sex experience, except perhaps for lonely, straight roads and Indianapolis 500 veterans. But the act does illustrate the importance of the place in which we carry out our sexual activities. If you and your partner feel you have tried just about everything possible between one another to the extent that knocking off a surreptitious piece on your suburban roof has become a routine midnight adventure, perhaps you need a change of scene or some new devices to heighten the excitement. There are many artifical aids, sex toys, and outside influences which can heighten sex, which in a way is a form of exploration, "sexploration," and sometimes calls for the zest and daring of the adventurer.

Going to a different bedroom, especially to the kind of luxurious room that is padded with invitingly furry carpeting, mirrors for greater self-visibility, with warm red lighting —perhaps candlelight flickering, velvet walls and satin sheets all can turn you on like a fountain. A Roman bath, a sauna, the attic or kitchen table, or have you ever tried the lawn in the backyard? How about the beach sands, the surf, or a mountain-top, a boat or a train, face-to-face on horseback, or via bicycle?

One couple told me of a special thrill they found in the snow. He loved tobogganing, especially if the hill was long enough. She would sit in front, and once they had started downhill, she would hike up the back of her ski jacket, bunch her slacks and panties down, and sit on the erection he produced from his frosty fly. Fresh air is good for you. However, after the excitement of the first time, it usually took them two hills to really make it big. Don't ever try it on skis, recommend our same two outdoor advisers, unless you want to wind up in splints. On the other hand, you may discover a mountain cabin with a fireplace.

For warmer sites, there are tent floors and hammocks, and the wide out-of-doors by a campfire. I would not dare be so commonplace as to suggest such routine sex locales as swimming pools, and spots like icy mountain streams and waterfalls can turn you off unless you're accustomed to frigid showers. However, we will never snub any sexual excitement on the grounds that it may be prosaic. Some couples who have become strapped and sapped by routine report excellent results in just the simple, memory-provoking activity of taking the family car, parking it in a dark place and climbing in the back seat. It does something to girls who remember all the times they were there and didn't.

The imagination must be brought into play. The proper mixture of the peril and penalties of being caught, along with the excitement of newness, near exhibitionism, daring, memory, or even outrage must be discovered by each couple. For example, making it on the beach or in the woods can be thrilling, and women especially love the back-to-nature trip. But, do you care about binoculars, voyeurs in the bushes or possible interlopers aroused to the extent of turning your adventure into a forced multiple experience or worse? It may be spectacular to roll naked in a vacant stadium or football field, but what about the watchman, or breaking and entering laws? The idea is, even when you throw caution to the winds, you wouldn't want anything to disrupt the sport that is the aim of the whole thing. A little cowardice is the manly thing in such a case. The prudent rooftop lay is the best rooftop lay.

One couple I know do a lot of babysitting for their friends and neighbors. It gives this lovable housewife's perverse little suburban mind a special secret smile in later visits to know she and her husband have made it on the table where she is enjoying coffee with the girls, or on top of the television console their friends watch every night. They even take explicit pictures with their little Polaroid kit and have an excellent album which they keep under lock and key like some people keep their vacation slides.

Photographic pornography can be an excellent aid to heightening the excitement of sex, which reminds me of a friends's experience, which he recounted with the profound regret that it was impossible to photograph. He had taken his girlfriend to a very elegant cocktail lounge which he frequented, one of those plush places resplendent with rich woods, leather upholstery and deep carpets. It was late in the evening and there were only a few strangers around the bar. As a matter of habit he took up his stance down the far end, around the curve of what was the common, backwards-C-shaped bar. He ordered martinis for them both and, standing with a foot on the rail while she spun on a swivel chair beside him, exchanged a few pleasantries with the bartender, who drifted off to continue a conversation with the other couples after an interval. He made some remark to his girl, who did not answer, and so he turned to see that she was gone. His immediate thought was that she must have gone to the ladies room. Then he felt the tug at his zipper and became alarmedly aware of where she was and what she was doing. Despite his hushes, protests and mixed delight, she took out his penis and, crouched down behind the bar, started sucking him, while he tried to hang on and look casual with a furtive sip at his drink, desperately playing the lookout.

In the unusual, but familiar surroundings, where under the stimulation of drink he had often thought about the joys of sex, it was all over in an instant. He tried not to change the expression on his face, but at the very end there was one extra large gulp he could not stifle, and his girl *did* have to go to the ladies room at that point. Needless to say, when he got her home that night he rewarded her with an enthuisasm as though they were starting out on a whole new sex life.

Why is it that such bizarre experiences are so intriguing? Because they heighten the awareness of reality. Everyone sooner or later becomes jaded to his surroundings, and this can sadly apply also to our bodies and the bodies of those closest to us. If you move into a house on a highway where there are vehicles roaring by all night, chances are they will disturb your sleep at first. Later, the mind becomes used to them and you don't consciously hear them. That can happen to couples and their lovemaking unless they learn to innovate. The man must always keep his eyes and other senses attuned for that instant in a woman's life when she needs something new and rare, and he must make it new. Capture the imagination of an excitable woman and you'd be surprised; for a thrill she will lay you in a Boeing 747–14 bathrooms!—or eat you on the patio of your motel room, while you stand there, visible from the waist up, looking at hundreds of people around you. And if *you* don't excite her with such wild ideas, maybe somebody else will.

The place, the scene and setting, the variations and the experimentation are of unremitting importance in any thorough sexploration of two people. I remember when I was very young a teenage girl was showing me some routine snapshots of herself, the usual thing, standing there looking at the camera in a variety of settings, a park, the school, her street. One photograph, however, she tried to hide, and I later peeked at it. It showed her in a very normal pose, fully clothed, and staring right at the camera. I was about to brush it aside with the conclusion that she had not liked her expression or posture and had hid it for that reason.

Then I noticed. One hand dangled at her side. The other, with the index finger, almost touched the crotch. The significance of that gesture, the photographing it, told worlds about her. It said she was aware, and intrigued by the reality of her body and the aperture at her crotch. Since somebody had to take the picture, it indicated she wasn't afraid of experimenting with her body. I got laid that night.

Except for the use of mirrors, which can

be very effective in exciting the passions, most of us do not know what we look like, and especially don't know how we look when we are engaged in sex. Self photography, of the safe, Polaroid type as described earlier, can be an excellent turn-on. You can even use the camera to build into an exceedingly hot passion by taking several naked pictures of your partner first, and having her photograph you in all your arousal before posing together and using a cable release extension or a timer for tripping the shutter. The interruptions, the periodic viewing of yourselves in action can make the whole experiment an explosive one. You can save the photos for future turn-ons.

Females, particularly ones who have led sheltered lives, love pornography. If you live within a thousand miles of a city where such books can be purchased or where such films are shown, it will be a rewarding trip. Most major cities from coast to coast now have "art house" type theaters where films are shown in full color, although with very poor scripts, which display every possible erotic action between male and female in explicit detail. Usually the actors are young, good-looking people with healthy, alluring bodies, totally liberated sexual drives and more than a slight touch of exhibitionism, even though they'll all say they do it for the money.

If your partner is unaware of the diversities of the flesh or how commonly they are practiced, such exposure may turn her on for some experimentation. In any event, every sensuous male should at least see one, preferably with a girl. If you fear entering such theaters, you tremble unnecessarily. Most of them are clean, comfortable, dark places. They are usually under the watchful eye of the law, which would love to shut them down for Health Department or vice infractions but hasn't been able to come up with charges that the Supreme Court doesn't reject. They sell popcorn, too. You won't see John Wayne and Raquel Welch performing, though—not this year, anyway.

If you are too shy to take a girl to such a theater, and can't muster up the pose of being an indignant spy for the PTA, you can always buy reels of pornographic films from stores which are advertised usually as "Adult Book Stores," a phenomenon also sweeping the country and strictly legal. Such places and films most often are advertised in the so-called "underground newspapers," and since these are also the contacts for purchasing exotic devices and sex tools, you must be able to locate one. If you cannot locate an underground newspaper in your own city try a nearby metropolis.

As for novelties, we have mentioned in the appropriate chapters the devices for masturbating and such fields of play as the water bed. Vibrators are one sex tool that should be part of every well-stocked sex room. They are available, in most drug stores in fact, in two different basic models. One of them, obviously designed for plunging the depths of sex but always advertised innocuously as a personal facial skin vibrator, costs only a few dollars and is shaped exactly like the human penis, except for certain ridges and coloring. The batteries are contained within, and the switch is on the flat end. Moisture proof, since the instrument really was designed for insertion in the female vagina, they have a bullet-rounded head and dimensions of the average erect penis. There are two sizes available, but don't take your girl in—drug stores usually don't have fitting rooms.

The other model of vibrator, which consists of small motor, wrist strap and attachments, also does a good deal more for a woman than for a man, either placed inside her, teasing her clitoris, or on her breasts. For arousing the animal inside a woman, there's nothing like them. One friend told me of applying the tubular variety to a girl's breasts and pubis until she was so inflamed with erection of the nipples and clitoris that she lunged for him physically, leaping on his own living, irreplaceable penis. The hand-strapped vibrator permits a male to use his fingers in vital areas of the woman with a mechanized massage that excites even the most fatigued flesh.

I was told of an incident at a swinging party, which seemed to be over, when everyone was sitting, clothed in the living room of the private home, sharing a drink and conversation in the early hours of the morning. One thin girl with short-cropped blonde hair had, however, stretched out naked in a state of total collapse behind the sofa, which formed a kind of passageway between it and the wall, leading to the bedroom areas where the blonde evidentally had spent too much time. Noise was made, drinks were offered, even the chilliness of the evening failed to disturb her profound sleep until the host, donning a hand vibrator, reached down and put his fingers into her crotch. In two minutes she was moaning and stirring, and in three minutes she was dragging him back into the bedroom area.

There are numerous attachments that can delight and help satisfy the most demanding woman. Attachments of soft pink plastic fit over the penis as an extension, elongating it and enlarging it. There is also a device which fits over the penis like a hollow phallus or dildo but, being designed for those who have trouble maintaining an erection, it only inflates to full rigidity when the penis softens. When the penis is engorged and swollen it relaxes and lets the natural organ do the work.

Several varieties of the so-called "French tickler" also are available. One of these is a feather-type extension that fits at the top of the penis on a soft elastic band and is able to delicately stimulate the very mouth of the cervix at the deep end of the vagina, a great thrill to women who have never been penetrated so deeply. There are also band-type ticklers which are flesh-colored elastic, fitting around the penis like wide rubber bands and surfaced with numerous small nodes or teats that excite the sides of the vagina, touching off nerves that have never been reached inside her and making the penis seem wider. A similar brand runs lengthwise along the penis for maintaining tantalizing contact with the clitoris at every thrust. Women say it feels like being penetrated by a horney giant. The soft pressure which the bands apply to the penis itself, in addition to the women's extra excitement and the unusual feeling of an artificial extension, can make the experiment volcanic.

Dildoes of every possible size, from cross-legged virgin to baseball bat, some of them perfectly sculptured to match every ridge of the human penis, can also be employed as devices to heighten the sexual experience. A female who has been ravished by a full-capacity plastic dildo before you enter her, is ready to climb to a new plateau under the urging of your arousedly competitive organ of flesh; in fact, she may climb the bedroom walls.

One word about other sex items. There are many potions and other edibles which are reputed to be aphrodisiacs on the market in America, but none can be regarded as safe, so none is recommended. If your female starts taking her clothes off after two martinis, or a similar high is reached, you are lucky; alcohol is the only legal and unharmful thing which can do it. Almost every device mentioned, including films, usually is available through your friendly corner "dirty book" store, or through the ads mentioned. If perchance there is some far frontier of the nation where such things have not penetrated, write for advertised catalogs of what they legally call "novelties."

Of course the inventive mind can devise many sex-heightening articles and procedures on its own—"Darling, it occurred to me that I'd like to insert the living room lamp in your vagina!"—but efficiency in sex does not depend on external gadgets but more effective use of the organs that you possess.

CHAPTER XV

SEX GAMES THAT GROUPS PLAY

Many people feel that a one-to-one sexual relationship is the most intense and ideal. This contention is not to be disputed, for a whole world of sex exploration is possible in the chemistry that two people can fire up together. In fact, the majority of people live their entire lives without ever realizing the deepest possiblities for sex appreciation and mutual pleasure which can be attained between one male and one female.

But if we consider that two people can learn to fly together in a feat of sexual levitation, the true sensualist sets his mind free and ponders the idea of group sex, perhaps a three-some at first, then on to an orgy, which might be likened to the space travel of the sexual world. Orgies and group sex are an intriguing subject to most people. Those who do participate are intrigued as to why others don't. People who don't participate are mystified and sometimes repulsed by people who do practice such activities.

Whatever your feelings regarding such

practices, and this is not a testimonial in favor of them, you should know that such erotic pursuits are not limited to the pages of hard-core pornography, intimate histories of Rome, or houses of prostitution. There are thousands of orgies occuring in America every weekend night, and millions of men and women have experienced sex on this level. They may be the ones you see walking around smiling with secret satisfaction all week long. Often they are beautiful, daring people; they come from all walks of life. On the other hand, anyone's first experience with group sex may be traumatic, disillusioning and soul shattering.

When you remove your clothes and step into a group of a half dozen other naked persons of both sexes, all intent on sexual delight, you lay your ego on the line. If you have any insecurities about the size of your penis, the depth of your erotic prowess, your ability to please and perform, in fact any competitive hangups at all, you can practically be assured that your role will be limited to that of voyeur due to a shrivelling psychological mechanism known as innate fear.

For any male truly desirous of fulfilling his sensuality potential to the outer limits, group sex is something that should be considered. Think about it a few moments if you have never experienced an orgy or a group sex act. Investigate your feelings. Are you repulsed? Are you curious? Or are you just blank? At least your mind is not closed to the idea. It may not be your bag, but it doesn't bother you that others do it. Interested?

Perhaps the best way for the uninitiated to explore his curiosity regarding orgies or group sex is to experience it for the first time as a voyeur. There are situations in which this is permitted, common in fact, and we will suggest two approaches below. But, considering yourself a voyeur, let me describe to you a few typical group sex experiences from my own research. Try to put yourself into the scene and see how you would react.

The following description of group sex, although not categorically a true orgy, is an interesting and explicit one, taken from an only slightly edited tape recording by a quite literate party who was volunteering his personal experience specifically for this book, not as a patient. He was among the first to discover a sort of sex ranch where group sex was a regular occurrence. He and his girl had been to a dinner party at the ranch and had lingered over wine and conversation until only a foursome was left at the table. Both couples were more interested at that point in private communion, but the only question was where they could go to make love. His story picks up at that crossroads of the early evening:

"The other couple we had been talking to proceeded with their sex play pretty openly, so that we got the idea they had claimed the room we were in. We walked off, hand in hand, going from one room to another, looking for privacy. In the kitchen several couples were mixing drinks. We looked in and I went a bit wide-eyed at spotting, over in a corner on the counter, a girl sitting there, her arms gripping her knees. She smiled at my intrusion and ruffled the hair on the male who was in the process of eating her. We tried all the doors to other rooms but they were either locked or otherwise signified their occupancy via the groans or squeaks filtering through them.

"One door led down to the basement on a carpeted stairway. There were few lights at the bottom. We became quickly aware, however, that there were people all around, viewed only in flashes as though lit up by their bodies alone. One couple lay stretched full length in the corner, sixty-nining. Beside them a girl was sitting on a man's lap, which would be a very normal party-type position except for the strained expression on her face—she was impaled on six or eight inches of him. A light at the end of the room seemed inviting. We stepped in there and at first we were disappointed, because it looked like we had entered a dead-end bathroom and, dammit, there was no lock on the door. But our search seemed successful because just beyond the bathroom, on the other side, there was a large room, lighted and empty, with mattresses spread wall to wall.

"We got undressed and planted our clothing like flags of occupation for what we intended to be a long and leisurely love-making session. The urgency of sex was gone because we had had each other as a pre-dinner appetizer, so we could afford to lay there and toy with one another to build up in our bodies a full hour's glow of sexuality strong enough to make us come just from the extra excitement of looking into each other's eyes. I rubbed her back and her shoulders and her rump, a real beauty of an ass—almost a Hottentot, from this thrusting-humping exercise she had been doing since she was sixteen. She caressed me, too, knowing I love the light feel of butterfly fingers flickering and descending and teasing from my neck to my knees, a touch somewhere between a tickle and a gentle breeze on the skin.

"I was inside her when the first other couple came in. I kept stroking long, careful, tender strokes, the full length in and out, stirring her clitoral pool of moisture momentarily with the tip of my organ on each withdrawal before surging back into her with a lunge that pressed our bones together at the pubis; inside I must have been jostling the mouth of her womb. The other couple, a tall, bearded, musician named Dan and a supple Hawaiian we called Looloo, barely glanced at us and went about their business one mattress distant from us. My girl wasn't the least disturbed at sharing the bedroom at this point, and, in fact, I found it exciting too to see Looloo go down on Dan briefly, unhesitatingly, as naturally as children at play.

"Then *another* couple marched in and took up space on the other side of them.

None of us were touching, it was one mattress per couple, but we were close enough to see the swinging of their bodies in reaction to one another, to hear the slapping of flesh against flesh in the case of the newcomers, and to hear the sounds of sucking and kissing and screwing, and the sighs and groans. We could smell other bodies working up a love sweat amid all the strange perfumes and lotions the participants wore. We realized, my girl and I, that we hadn't just been lucky to discover an empty room, but had mistakenly started off what was the regular Saturday night event of mass sex that took place in that room.

"The next entry was a foursome, three males and one woman who occupied the entire wall perpendicular from us. They were engaging in something special. The woman, a dusty-haired slim girl with drooping breasts, began sucking the penis of one man who sat on his ankles, leaning against the far wall and supporting her head on his thighs. A second guy—she was face down—entered her from a kneeling position into her vagina, which jacked her lower body up a little, although she wasn't really up on her knees. The third guy, who we later learned was her husband, squatted against the wall behind the guy screwing his wife and, with a can of beer in his hand, watched the whole process, even getting down on his fours at some points to squint for a closeup of the in-out motion. Because of their positions, every thrust into the woman's vagina pushed her whole body, and her head, down on the other man's penis. Another couple came in naked—he limping from a cast on his leg—and sat down at the end of the room, each with a drink, obviously not intending to do anything but watch. Unfortunately, as I said earlier, the room was right next to the bathroom, which gradually got real busy with flushing sounds, conversations between girls, and even one girl nagging her man. That, and the fact that the voyeur couple didn't even have the decency to shut up—they carried on a loud conversation as though they were in a bowling alley discussing World War II—was a big turn-off.

"Altogether it was very distracting. If the lighting had been a little dimmer, so that all you saw was a sea of bodies enjoying separate sex, with their noises, vocal and otherwise, it could have really turned me on, I thought. My girl, lying therc panting at every thrust, later told me she did get a kind of warm, cosmic sense out of it, a feeling of sharing, going through the motions that humans everywhere go through struggling to get closer. She felt this sensation of sharing. She liked the sounds of other's coming, the sighs and moans. She said she had an urge to take Looloo's hand when she was coming. But, particularly with the voyeurs, as I said, it wasn't as stimulating for me as it might have been under different conditions. I mean, it would have helped if we knew ahead of time. Since there *was* a distracting influence, though, it did delay my orgasm longer than usual, much longer, and with my girl begging me to come by that time, really enjoying my longevity, I finally exploded in one of my best sex explosions of the year. So I shared too, despite myself."

End of story. Well, that was not really an orgy, just a matter of people practicing sex individually in the same room. If it had been a regular orgy—even though there is no national association which has established guidelines for qualifying—there would have been more interaction between the couples.

Orgies can consist of any number of people, from two couples on up to any number, as many as space permits. Someone could rent a stadium if they had the funds and the participants. Your average, run-of-the-mill, everyday type of orgy consists of between four and six couples and is a scene in which a male often may feel threatened. More often than not, it is females who contrive or arrange these orgies. They do it because in such a situation, there is nothing wrong with their making it with another female, according to an unspoken code, although they might never go off into a room alone with another female.

Certain females, popularly called bi's because they can get their sexual thrills either with a man or woman, quickly make their selection known in an orgy scene. Many times, it is merely a case of a woman wanting to take the singular opportunity of broadening her range of experience; if she has never been "done"—orally stimulated by another female—she might want to try the sensation either actively, in sixty-nine, or passively, in sixty. Bi's are not necessarily lesbians. Usually they are married or sexually involved with males but—semantics aside—are sexually liberated enough to wish to try everything that sends vibrations through their loins.

Many males are able to get over the first hump of orgy experience by becoming a voyeur. If this isn't your bag, you can stimulate some female who is already occupied by stroking or penetrating her anus or caressing her breasts. No one in an orgy is going to jump up and scream, "Don't you dare," unless some violent activity is thrust upon them unawares or something disturbs their obvious total satisfaction with what they're doing. Likes and dislikes in the orgy are usually shown by body motion rather than words. If you offer your penis to a female either orally or at the other end, she will either take it or roll aside to a different embrace.

At times, for varied reasons, all members of an orgy will spontaneously decide to turn on one member of the group. Sometimes it isn't a matter of spontaneity exactly, but just a matter of each person by turn. If it's a female member the game is called Queen of the May and if it's a male it's known as King of the Mountain.

Let me describe a typical orgy of this nature, with a female on the bottom, lying there with her legs stretched out and her arms over her head in the middle of a king-size bed. A woman has more sexual equipment, so it's more interesting. Besides, in the case of a woman, both males and females stimulate her, while in the case of a man, it's restricted to members of the opposite sex.

The girl lies there with her hair fanned out under her head while one person bends and soul-kisses her, busying her lips and obscuring her body from her own view so that she will concentrate on feeling. Two other persons stimulate her breasts, teasing the nipple with a finger or bending to suck it, molding the soft flesh. One person kneels to perform cunnilingus at her crotch while a hand reaches under from somewhere, stimulating her anus. Someone else strokes her thighs, and one or two men place a penis into her hands at different intervals. There are variations. A man may place his penis within reach of her mouth, or a woman may extend her crotch in the same way, straddling her face if she indicates a wish to kiss it.

When it's the man's turn for King of the Mountain, the girls surround him as he lies back, ready for fantasyland. Every wish is their command. One of them may suck his penis while another bends over him with her vagina. They change around and the stimulations come from all directions. One kisses your lips while another kisses your penis and another stimulates your anus. Two others may lick your nipples and other parts of your body, your ears or your thighs. It's like making it in the dark with a girl who has a dozen hands and tongues. A gigantic climax is not unusual, with some member of the stimulating party often mounting the enlarged male to catch his final moments of passion, somewhere around four on the Richter scale.

If all this sounds a little too much for you, maybe you could start small with a threesome. It works well if you can involve a girl who you know really turns you on sexually, or your wife, if she fits the bill and is willing. It's not something to spring on any girl out of the blue. Take your time and make the right choice. The second girl should be someone you both find stimulating. While you don't need a scorecard, perhaps some little diagrams will help. The couple with the basic relationship will be A and B, respectively, the male and the female who are accustomed to one another, while the third female will be designated as C.

A orally stimulates C's vagina while B kisses C's mouth and then her breasts. C performs fellatio on A while B is digitally stimulating C's anus and vagina. C kisses B's mouth and breasts while A is inserting his penis into C's vagina. Once actual intercourse takes place between A and C, B is free to stimulate A's anus or kiss B's breasts or mouth.

Numerous variations are possible, as diverse as the anatomy and imagination of the persons involved. Sometimes, in large groups of couples, the participants will work in a circle, with every man sucking a woman and being sucked by a different woman, but this kind of clockwork is the exception rather than the rule, usually requiring an agreement beforehand. Most orgies are rather spontaneous. If you have no idea where you might witness one, there are two possibilities. Buy a good color film showing multiple sex for study in the privacy of your home, or get in touch with the Sexual Freedom League, which is known to sponsor gatherings which may often turn into orgies. Legally, of course, they do not assemble for that purpose but rather for discussion of lofty subjects of redeeming merit. These discussions, varying in length from one to several thousand words, generally arouse the participants. Again a case of semantics and the law.

One last word on orgies. A tall, big-boned blonde who sexually was as wide open as a volcano told me how she was introduced to the orgy scene by a boyfriend who had left his wife because she refused to join in sex with others. It was something he had to have; it really turned him on. But the girl complained that, even though their own sexual relationship was fabulous on a one-to-one basis, whenever they got into an orgy group, he would try to direct her activities, always placing her into the position of forcing a female crotch into her mouth or a female's head into her crotch.

This quite liberated girl saw nothing

wrong with an occasional experience of that nature, but she greatly disliked the idea of someone else deciding for her what her sexual experience would be. Since he always tried to put her into bi-sexual lovemaking, she concluded, he was actually acting out, through her, his own latent homosexuality. This is probably true. While it would have been unacceptable even in an orgy scene for him to engage in sex with another male, vicariously he could dare to participate by viewing someone he was close to and loved in a comparable love-making situation.

This is a curious thing about our sexual society. While it is permissible for two females to kiss and caress and make love, and in fact is often encouraged, it is considered an outrage that two males might think of the same thing. In our sometimes illogical culture, where the female form, particularly the breasts, is used to sell everything from tractors to plumbing supplies, we are conditioned so that both males and females admire feminine anatomy. But with males, there is almost a morbid fear of touching, lest someone might think they're "gay." So the sight of two females making love is not repulsive to the male, while viewing two males making love might evoke disgust and revulsion. As hangups or fears of homosexuality may constrict sexuality, steps should be taken to be aware of them and set them aside.

CHAPTER XVI

FEARS ABOUT MALE SEXUALITY

One of the most puzzling cases I have ever encountered as a psychologist occurred several years ago in New York, and, for all I know, is still occurring there. A woman came to me and described a problem. "I've been living with a man for quite a while, and we get along together pretty well except for one thing," she said. "We found a nice third floor apartment and I've got it fixed up real comfortable, and he doesn't drink or beat me up or anything. He's awful nice. The only thing is . . . when it comes to sex, there's only one way he can do it, and I tell you, it gets pretty rough. The only way is, I have to strip naked and lie down on a solid cake of ice and he gets on top of me; that's the only way he does it!"

Hiding my professional eyebrow raising at this bizarre practice but still probing for further details, I got her to reaffirm what she had said. They spread out what actually was a bed of ice, then she lay back, he mounted her and pumped until he came. The sheer logistics of it seemed overwhelming. Can you imagine first of all even finding an ice man in these days of refrigeration, and then asking him to haul all that ice up three flights of stairs to an apartment? What did they do when it melted, or how did they get rid of it afterwards? That puzzling part I was never able to figure out.

She always went along with his desires, she indicated, without questioning. The image of the two of them copulating on melting ice on the third floor of a New York apartment building is one of those hilarious thoughts that never fail to bring a chuckle. But she even added a punch-line. She had been going through with this chilling romance all along, and she asked, "Tell me, do you think there's something wrong with him?"

With *him?* Nothing wrong with him except a touch of necrophilia, a trace of latent homosexuality and what I would guess would be a chronic case of cold penis, but the question to the woman was, "What's *your* bag?"

Psychologists are asked to examine all kinds of cases involving frigidity, but this was something that wasn't in the textbooks. If only I could have documented it, like talking to that ice man, to discover just what he thought when they said, "Yes, we ordered eight blocks of ice. Just spread them out on the floor over there . . ."

Seriously though, the case does have a couple of points I wanted to bring up. First, there are some pretty strange ways of making love in America and second, when the problem is sexual, it's almost always the woman who comes for therapy, not the man. In fact, my office practice was a constant flow of rather attractive women with sexual difficulties of some sort or another.

We have to admit that there are a lot of sexual hangups going around, and the first scientist to come up with a wonder drug to cure them all is going to make millions and be enshrined in immortality. The Nobel Peace Prize, at least, because people who are content with their sex lives are notorious pacifists.

However, as things stand in our culture, it is easier for a female to admit that her sex life is not all that she wants it to be than it is for a male. For a male to admit the possibility that he may not be the world's greatest lover is considered a blow to his masculinity.

It begins from his earliest days and the parental coaxing, "Be a man, son." Through the teenage years he learns to lie about conquests so that if some other liar boasts of seven consecutive orgasms without losing his erection, the youth will up him to ten. To play poker with the boys, to go hunting with a symbolic penis that echoes its prowess through the canyons, to fight in an army, to participate in the thrill of he-man sports of grunting body contact, these are all considered manly. A man can be strong and silent, and this is considered admirable. If he sits alone at nights, lonely and sexually unfulfilled, he is at least admirable for suffering in silence. So the men, fearful of the slightest taint on their virility, let the women, who are after all the custodians of love and all things warm and soft, seek out the answers.

It is changing a bit with the new generation, where we have men brave enough to wear long hair and lacey clothes and say to hell with what the "guys" think. Since the hippies have a storied proclivity for free love, sex orgies and that sort of thing, they can get away with it, because at least they aren't fairies.

There is probably nothing which brings as much horror to the mind of complacent middle class American males as the possibility that somebody might think them queer, a fag, a homo, a queen. The fear is one of the deepest rooted ones in the culture, and sweeps the socio-economic scale from bottom to top. Even the most liberal of sexualists have some reservations regarding homosexuality.

Let me tell you about my own experience attending a sex orgy. It was at one of the more conservative sex clubs, where orgies are never scheduled and if and when they happen it is strictly a spontaneous affair. Girls are much freer about letting themselves go and diving into the activity of a sex orgy than males. However, I considered it my duty to investigate the phenomenon at least from the point of view of broadening experience, or to chalk it up to research. Those two statements are, of course, masculine lies. The real reason for my interest in the orgy was a certain blonde with peaches and cream skin and perfect, seductive features. She had big, pouted lips and a smouldering quality. Another girl, a black-haired beauty straight out of the islands, who even walked with a sensual stealth as though she were climbing a coconut tree barefoot to perform some sexual experiment atop, suggested that the six of us in a group, three men and three women, strip and—well, a certain president's phrase might be misquoted: "Let us come together . . ."

Great, I thought, maneuvering next to the blonde and figuring that even if somebody beat me to her, that dark haired girl was something else again. I stripped, then turned to dive into the two king-size beds which had been pushed together for the event. My eyes quickly caught the blonde. She was making out already, sixty-nining it with the dark-haired girl. The other two men were into the same girl and there was no place for my rejected sex organ to go, so it went limp. Talk about a shock to the ego. There are two beautiful women who both have the opportunity of experiencing *me*, and they can't wait to get at each other. This frequently happens in orgies, and while it is considered very sexy for two girls to make out together, it is taboo for men to do the same. That would be homosexual!

Even when couples are making out on the same bed, several men with several women in a situation where multiple body contact heightens the sensation of group activity, you will see that if a male happens to bump against a male, both tend to pull quickly apart in a movement that attests, "I certainly didn't mean anything by that–"

The truly sensual male must become comfortable enough with his own masculinity that he is not carrying around any fears with him. Since the fear of homosexuality is so widespread, let's have a few words about it so that we can see that we need not fear. Any fear that you bring to bed with you can spoil your experience there, because if you have a fear you are hiding, then you can't completely let go, can you?

Concerning patterns of sexual behavior, a great deal of thinking done by scientists and laymen alike stems from the assumption that there are persons who are "heterosexual," or straight, and persons who are "homosexual," or gay–those whose sexual inclinations are toward persons of the same sex. The assumption–and nobody is taught otherwise because it's a subject nobody even discusses–is that these two types represent antitheses in the sexual world—that you're either one or the other—and that there is only an insignificant class of "bisexuals" who occupy an intermediate position between the other guys. It is implied that every individual is innately or inherently either heterosexual or homosexual, or by popular terminology, normal or queer, depending on the method he uses in coming off. It is further implied that from the time of birth one is fated to be one thing or the other, and there is little chance for one to change this pattern in the course of a lifetime.

The current research in psychology and psychiatry makes it apparent, however, that the heterosexuality or homosexuality of many individuals is not an all-or-none proposition. There are people whose histories are exclusively homosexual, both in experience and inner fantasies. But the record also shows that a considerable portion of the population have combined within their individual histories both homosexual and heterosexual experiences and/or fantasy responses. There are some whose heterosexual experiences predominate and some whose homosexual experiences predominate, and some who have had quite equal amounts of both experiences.

We must recognize that males do not represent two distinct and separate populations, heterosexual and homosexual. The world is not to be divided into sheep and wolves. Only the human mind invents categories and tries to force facts into separated pigeon-holes.

Every psychologist who has ever been associated with the American prison system has heard some variation of the following comment from a convict: "My cellmate is a homosexual." Oh, the psychologist asks, how do you know, and the convict replies, "He blew me last night," or, "I stuck it up his ass last night." It is odd how the mind can separate the fact that when two persons engage in some homosexual act, they engage in it together, with some degree of voluntary participation. It has been estimated that at some age or another, the majority of males in America, as well as females, have been involved in some sort of homosexual act or other. This does not mean they are homosexuals. It means they are fairly normal people.

It might even be argued that those who have not experienced some sort of homosexual incident in their lives, since the incidence of such experience is so high, have avoided it and may be suspected of latent homosexuality by virtue of the fact that they must have taken great pains to avoid such contact.

The living world actually is a continuity of all gradations and mixtures of homosexual and heterosexual. We must accept this and the sooner we do the sooner we shall reach a sound understanding of the realities of sex. But sometimes it is like trying to explain black and white heredity. To certain persons who have been taught certain beliefs, a person is a Negro even if they are as white as an albino, if it happens that four generations back, one of their progenitors was knocked up by a Negro. Does this mean that if you decided one night, being a white man subjected to the provocation of a female who happened to be black, if you decided to lay her, you are a latent Negro? That's about as valid as our homosexual terminology. In reality categories are immaterial. In life we meet people, not categories.

If you have chosen the direction of the female as the point of expression of your sexual drive, then no matter what your past encounters may have been, you are functioning as a heterosexual.

Psychotherapists know that homosexuals are not born, but made, that genetic, hereditary, constitutional, glandular or hormonal factors have no significance in causing homosexuality. Environmental influences are the determining forces which affect our choices of sexual partners. If your adult identity is heterosexual, then sexual experiences with males will not change this identity, but probably will further your own masculine image. Whether or not you are turned on by the stock market, the sports pages, or the latest issue of *Field and Stream* also are factors which do not determine your sexuality.

Males with a life-long history of withdrawn behavior, feelings of isolation, detachment, or inability to form effective relationships with either family or friends will tend to be the least sensuous males. The man who fears being hurt, who has no gender or erotic identity, and is persistently anxious in social contact or interaction, still is able to achieve some degree of sensuality. Conversely, the male with a history of gregariousness, warmth, and affectionate behavior in or outside the home with peers, siblings, relatives and others, has the best chance of being a truly sensuous male.

A careful examination of the male's self-image during significant periods of prepuberty, adolescence and early childhood can point out this role. For example, ask yourself a key question: Which image occurs to you of your role during masturbation and at the point of orgasm? At such times a very clear view of how the person sees himself sexually can be obtained by an honest answer.

Perhaps the poorest sensuality to develop in a man occurs when a person feels he always had a sense of himself as a female and has never desired to be male, or when he feels envious of females and desirous of being in their role in a sexual situation. Even then, seemingly defensive or counterfeit attempts at maleness nevertheless indicate some degree of heterosexual sensuality. At least the person's efforts have been directed at preserving his male indentity or acquiring whatever male identification he can.

Much of the insecurity of the masculine adult occurs because of restrictions and even educational taboos that prohibit duscussing the subect of sensuality. To check on statistics regarding male homosexual encounters in the heterosexual male, I just checked a popular sex manual currently being circulated. Even though the book, ostensibly covering both sexes, had a chapter regarding lesbianism, there was not a word on male homosexuality.

If sensuality is ever going to be fully realized in adulthood, then children are going to have to have the right, vocalized, to masturbate and to play sexually with other children. You cannot have sensuality without developing it, and you develop male or female sensuality by practice. You can create a lot of insecurities about sexuality by worrying about it, and that's what we have been doing for decades. Forget it. If you want to express yourself sexually inside the female body, seize your opportunities, and with a cry of delight, go to it. You are and are going to be the sum of your experience, nothing more. Be content with what you are, and keep experiencing.

CHAPTER XVII

SCIENCE AND THE "MERCY SCREW"

This chapter introduces as a contribution to the literature of sex and psychology a new term to describe what was yesteryear a rare happening between the sexes, yet a condition common to both sexes. A liberal-minded young blonde who came to me for therapy actually coined the phrase in describing her complaint, which basically stemmed from her lack of asserting her own personality. She was always finding herself getting involved with men she was not particularly attracted to. But whenever she did meet a man, she allowed herself—by lack of asserting her desires, being unwilling to disagree—invariably to wind up in bed with the guy. With a heavy sigh she declared, "I'm tired of these mercy screws!"

It often happens with men, too. An aggressive woman moves into a man's company at a party or in some other encounter. She smiles at him, displays her female accoutrements and voices words of invitation and interest. Being human, and therefore kind, and also not negligent of the factor of any person's humanity, the man talks, listens, and gets involved, even though he can see that the girl will not make the kind of sex partner he is seeking. But how can he snub her, without hurting her feelings and perhaps contributing to crippling her capacity as a sex partner for someone else? In certain situations a man must at least make a pass at a girl or he will be insulting her, and if by chance she accepts, then he must perform the "mercy screw."

The answer, of course, is for the sensuous male to be in charge right from the start and never let a situation get that far. To start with, as mentioned earlier, no matter what you have learned through years of exposure to toothpaste advertising, we must be very selective when it comes to smiling. Until he is sure of the situation, a male must be so noncommittal about his inclination toward sexual alliance that if the wrong woman more than casually shunted her thigh against his groin he would be able to say without offense, "Oh, pardon me, dear, I wasn't watching where I was going."

On the other hand, receptiveness on the part of females is a quality which can become quite exciting when shifted to the bedroom, so one must recognize that he might be passing up something good. Always remember that tomorrow is another day and the girl you do not go to bed with today may turn out to be an attractive possibility tomorrow, so no rejection should be handled with any finality. What we are considering here is a scene in which you wish to make your own choice and have not yet made it.

Before the conversational stage is reached, the sensual man must be able to observe. Supposing the scene is a party and people are standing around or sitting in little groups, sipping cocktails and talking. Visually, you can make some conclusions. Let your eyes drift around the room and study as many females as you can without getting trapped in a staring contest that someone might consider a signal of high interest. Look at all the women, not just the most ravishing beauty in the room, because the girl who takes the trouble to be the most perfect in dress and looks just might be the kind who is so unsure of herself that she has to have everything perfect.

Among the perils of beautiful women are the possibilities that she who has the most spectacular hairdo, most flashy dress and perfect form is someone who is afraid to rely on the power of her own personality to attract, and it is the *person* you must penetrate, not the adornments. Or she may pursue perfection to the point that she does not like to muss her hair in love-making and certainly doesn't want to get all sweaty. So many of the women who grew up with pretty-type faces have been babied and sweet-talked and protected to the extent that although they love the tribute of winning male attention, they don't wish to follow through to sexual expression. So dirty, you know.

On the other hand, many of the most beautiful girls start getting propositions at such an early age that they have become sexually mature earlier than their less attractive sisters. One of the best clues is in their motions. Is she listening to other people when they talk? Is she looking at them, thinking of what they say? Those are good signs. Does she have her arms folded or keep them closely restricted to her side? Bad. Does she move freely, easily, as though relaxed with her body? Ten points. Or if she's sitting, does she have her legs or ankles crossed and hands thrust into lap in a protective gesture? Those are bad signs. A woman who is comfortable with herself and her sexuality will tend to be open in gesture, will vocalize her thoughts and not be afraid to touch the people with whom she is in contact. The way she walks or holds herself can be interpreted to tell you if she is aware of what she has, is proud of it and willing to use it. If she lets her eyes seek out males elsewhere than the group she is in, chances are she is still available for an interesting encounter, looking for someone different to meet and talk to.

When you strike up a conversation, there are still clues to be picked up, whether you steer the conversation to food, dancing, politics or philosophy. People who like exotic foods tend to be the most sensual, and those who are interested in dancing indicate that they are not overly self-conscious of their bodies. When it comes to politics and philosophy, it isn't so much what they believe as how their minds work. Are they receptive and open-minded, or hostile to opposing arguments? Does she shock easily?

If you've gotten this far with a woman, you have exhibited an interest in her, and you must at no point in your talk ever let the idea that you are of the opposite sex be subordinated to any intellectual pursuit. Some men have an unfortunate way of saying to women, perhaps to protect themselves in fear of rejection, "I'm not really here talking to you because of your sex, I just like discussing ocean currents and would talk with anyone about it." No, you must press your questions and your answers to address the female, not the intellect. What your conversation should be directed toward communicating is the idea that, "I'm trying to discover as much as I can about your female quality so that I can see what kind of a couple we'd make sexually."

And while you are closely observing her, the fact to watch most closely for is this, is she observing you and sizing you up with a like curiosity? If so, you are probably in.

On the other hand, the male ego must be

strong enough to accept the possibility of occasional rejection by females, either because you are having an off night, are not coming across at your best, or, the poor fools are just making a horrible mistake. I remember when I was an adolescent and, only recently having discovered the amazing function of the human female, as though it was a private secret between me and all of them, my ego took a shattering bombardment every time I glanced at the women's pages of the newpaper. How could they? Why? I just couldn't understand it, how there were all these girls becoming engaged, spurning me, betraying me and getting married to other men, to do *it!*

The fact that they had never met me (and were not likely to) was no excuse for their outlandish perfidy, for how would they ever know what they were missing? Their faithlessness, their madness in dashing into those ill-advised but well publicized alliances hurt me deeply for a time until I stopped taking it as a personal rejection and decided to live and let live. After all, it takes all kinds. How could they know, anyway? Not everyone is bright enough to recognize greatness when they see it, and many girls make mistakes regularly, if you consider the rising marriage rates. This is the sort of attitude the male must maintain.

You can't win them all. Some girls are moved by their childhood, some by their experience, some by their frustrations, some by their aims, some by their intellect. Some things turn on some girls and turn off others. I met one girl recently who seemed to strike it off well with me. She was warm and receptive and we had a lot in common, apparently including a love for extensive worship at the pubic shrine.

Then it came to what I realized was her final exam question, the one point on which I was to either pass or flunk: 'What's your sign?" she demanded, and, even though I parried by trying to be vague in my answer, when I finally did reply, I lost. Our astrological signs didn't match, and that was it. According to her horoscope she was destined to lay someone with a different sign that night. Or maybe the whole month, for all I know. In any event, I am boning up on astrology because so many women chart their love lives by the sign of the zodiac today. If you don't know how to match your sign and hers—"Ah, but my moon is in the second house—" then it's like Russian roulette.

I met another girl who qualified the men in her life by professions. If the man were involved with a professional pursuit that intrigued her, she would sleep with him. Otherwise, no matter if he was the ideal in looks, manners, and everything else, if he didn't do the right kind of work, he was out. A lot of girls have their hangups. They will not come right out and say, "I only lay Democrats in election years," no, they just walk away.

The male, both in the pursuit and the resulting activities, must maintain his attitude as the penetrator, conversationally and sexually. If he's going to probe, prod, and stimulate in bed, then he's got to do the same thing on a different level in order to get there. He who knows what girls want (usually to be made aware that a man considers them singularly beautiful and desirable) will succeed most.

But getting back to the mercy screw. Those males who err will find themselves in the wrong bed, but it shouldn't happen too often. I remember one day when I was especially weary, to such an extent that I wasn't interested in sex, I believed. For relaxation and revival purposes I dove into a swimming pool and while floating there, minding my own business to the point of semi-coma, I was accosted by a female who—either due to my own feelings at the moment or whatever—did not particularly excite me. But talk about aggressive! I tried to drift away, and ended up being physically cornered by her, our bodies rubbing together in the shallow end of the pool, while my mind kept saying, "*No*, no, I don't want any more sex, I couldn't care less about sex."

On the other hand, while a man may smile to deceive, and may contrive the most fantastic lies and tell them with conviction, and can dress like a king or prince when he is nearly a pauper, there is one part of him that never lies. The most honest organ in your body is your penis. Despite all my intellectual protests that I did not want this girl, my sex organ began to contradict me and was taking a very firm position, if you'll forgive the pun.

So what starts out to look like a mercy screw may turn into something else again. It should be a point of honor with every sensuous male, as a member of the great confraternity of manhood, that he should be willing to lay any female that walks. To treat a woman callously, to deny her sexuality, is to damage the sex life of that person and some other male in the future by creating inhibitions. The mercy screw is in the last analysis a good deed to the sexual life of mankind, and the motto to keep in mind is, do unto others. Besides, it might be a lot better than you thought. Beauty is where you find it.

CHAPTER XVIII

SEX AND THE FUTURE

We are all traveling into the future, like it or not, and the future is a fascinating place. The one simple idea that in the future sexuality will be different has until now made it impossible to present a sensuality manual, especially one which is based on the radical concept that sex is fun. Sex *is* fun. In all my experience as a clinical psychologist and a human being I have not met one man, not one, who really believed that he engaged in sex for any other reason. Not for health, not for relief of tension, not for fulfilling the obligations of marital contracts, not for religious reasons, and certainly not for mere procreation of the race. It is one of the highest forms of communication, true, but if you want to say "I love you," do you really have to take her to bed?

The 1970s will probably be more notable in the story of man because of the liberation of the human spirit than for the construction of computer-controlled, power-thrusted vehicles capable of lunar exploration.

Man has always gazed at the moon, and his gazing did not inspire thoughts of rocketry, but of love. In the space of a few years (a white-smocked scientist, holding up a test tube, radiates success: he has discovered the Pill), with the fear of unwanted pregnancies diminished amidst a youth rebellion, more people have been making more love than ever before. Teenagers, hearing their parents warn against it, reached for the nearest warm female body to protest the Establishment. Older people, kept healthier by geriatric science, pursued the world's favorite recreation on crutches if necessary. And in between, mother and father investigated such burgeoning phenomena as social sex clubs.

Today on the screen in the major cities of the world you can view in full color the most explicit of sex acts in pubic close-up. Books and photographs called pornography are distributed everywhere. Even live sex performances, descending from the raw "exhibitions" put on in French whorehouses a generation ago, now can be seen on the stage in bars and theaters.

There are people who are alarmed at these developments, comparing them to the proliferation of nuclear weapons, or the tide of violence, crime, drugs and dissent sweeping everywhere. There will always be people alarmed at progress. We live in a society which has tried to repress any move in the direction of increased sexual expression by the people as though moral legislation was an unspoken mandate, part of the platform of every administration.

The duplicity of such a stance, the outright lie of it, can be seen not only in the fact that all governments declare a separation of religion and the state and admit that the morality of a people cannot be legislated, but also in the fact that they permit the entire economy to hinge on sex. They are saying that sex in advertising, a good deal of it pornography in disguise, is desirable, but the practice of sexuality is objectionable. No industry has a greater grasp of the mind of man than the advertising market researchers; and they are aware that men's and women's thoughts are sexual to the point of being pornographic.

But, except for the selling of mass-produced articles, we are told that sex is not good, especially too much sex, especially pornography. Our governments say so, our teachers say so, our ministers say so, and our parents say so. It is a matter of sexual policy. We have foreign policy, domestic policy and sexual policy: Sexual policy says sensuality is evil. It is argued that increased sensuality will result in the breakdown of the family unit, which is called the backbone of civilization. Yet existing sexual policy has resulted in the breakup of an estimated fifty percent of all marriages and has sent millions of vital people to mental institutions, crippled by conflicts between their feelings of sexuality and the concept that sensuality is evil. Millions of young people, seeing the obvious lie, have begun to suspect that there are a thousand other lies they are being told, and they are finding them and trying to blow them up, along with the absurdity that sensuality is evil.

Even then, broken homes, mental illness and rebellious youth are only part of the destruction stemming from the policy that considers sensuality evil. There are millions of lonely people in every corner of this most opulent country in the world, millions who ache over feelings of non-fulfillment and dream dreams of sex which for too many will never come true because it is too late. We must wonder how many people have died from a lack of wanting to live in a world that crushed their sexual hopes, a basic drive that left them disillusioned, and bereft of what should have been a major part of their lives, because everyone said sensuality is evil.

Ignoring sensuality is evil. Misery is evil. The pain of mental anguish and the crash of love that fails are evil. Deception and lies are evil. Wasting lives is evil. Sensuality is not evil.

Any psychologist from time to time tends to become depressed over witnessing the endless chain of people coming to him with lives bruised and battered in their conflicts about sex. I do not like to call people who come to me for therapy "patients," because what they are is fairly normal people with sexual problems, and if we call everybody with a sexual problem a patient, we are inferring that most of America had better line up for treatment. Actually, those who seek help with their problems are a lot healthier than those who don't, and this is probably the brightest, most optimistic, most visible trend in the annals of the human spirit. It is an endless cause for wonder and rejoicing that despite the repressive nature of their environment and the guilt associated with sex, people are exploring the sensual world with the indomitable spirit of pioneers.

It is up to each man to make himself aware of his sensual capabilities, and to pursue them, or risk an old age cursed by self-recriminations. It's the same as seeing a skyscraper going up and meeting an old man in rags who tells you, "I could have bought that piece of land twenty years ago for two hundred dollars!"

Think carefully about your powers and the penalty of wasting them, the possibility of regrets. There is a love feast going on in the world and the sensuous male will be guest of honor at the banquet. In order to get in (on the ground floor, as they say) you only have to recognize that a sexual revolution is taking place, a building boom in sensuality. And you must prepare yourself to join in.